Gobshite Quarterly

Double Trouble / Issue 13 – Winter 2014

This issue is dedicated to the memory of:

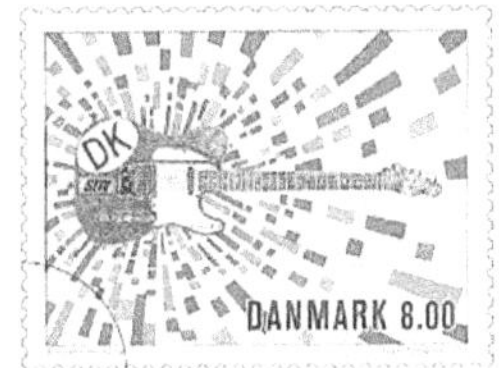

Zvonko Bušić (23 Jan., 1946 — 1 Sept., 2013)

Lou Reed (2 Mar., 1942 — 27 Oct., 27, 2013)

Zvonko Bušić (23 Jan., 1946 — 1 Sept., 2013)

Lou Reed (2 Mar., 1942 — 27 Oct., 27, 2013)

This issue is dedicated to the memory of:

Gobshite Quarterly

Double Trouble / Issue 14 – Spring 2014

9.00 USDOL || € 6.50 EURO || £ 5.30 GBP (UK) || $ 9.50 AUD (Oz) || $9.00 CAN || ¥ 870 JPY (japan yen) || 85.00 SAR (S. Africa)

9.00 USDOL || € 6.50 EURO || £ 5.30 GBP (UK) || $ 9.50 AUD (Oz) || $9.00 CAN || ¥ 870 JPY (japan yen) || 85.00 SAR (S. Africa)

Gobshite Quarterly

Double Trouble / Issue 13 – Winter 2014

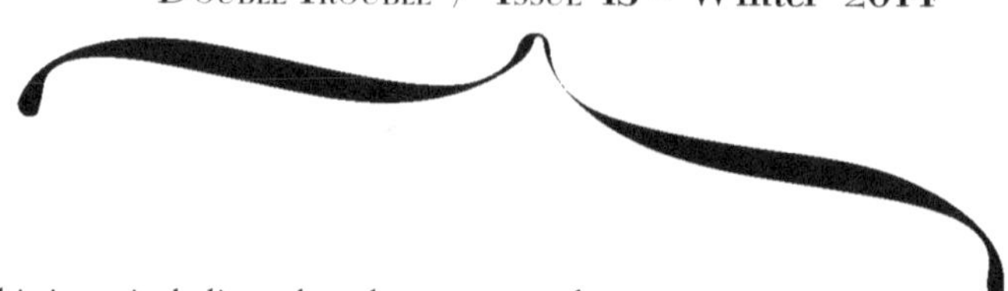

This issue is dedicated to the memory of:

Zvonko Bušić (23 Jan., 1946 — 1 Sept., 2013)
Lou Reed (2 Mar., 1942 — 27 Oct., 27, 2013)

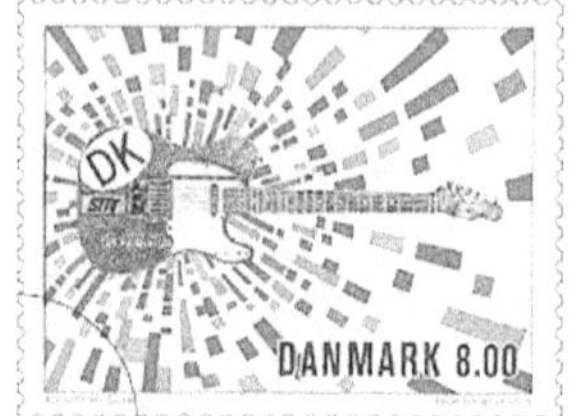

Portfolio / Spy Vs. Spy, photography, M. F. McAuliffe

The Usual Suspects
Staff

Editor R. V. Branham

Office Mgr. Sofia Sensei Satori Shostakovna Satyagraha Stolicniya Sashimi Shitkicker

Assoc. Editor M. F. McAuliffe

Contrib. Editors T. Warburton y Bajo & Channing Dodson & Arianna Morgan & Douglas Spangle

Design T. Warburton y Bajo

Cover Illo Graham K. Willoughby

Cover comix illos Sarah Laing & Wild eyed grp.

Photos M. F. McAuliffe, & T. Warburton y Bajo

Layout T. Warburton y Bajo & R. V. Branham

Design Assts. Channing Dodson & Arianna Morgan

Legal Peter Shaver

Publishers GobQ LLC/Reprobate Books

Post-production printing Ingram Spark/Lightning Source

P.R. P. H. Vazak

Gobshite Quaerterly: Double Trouble, Nos. 13/14, Winter & Spring 2014
ISBN 978-1-63068-139-5

Jean-Luc font by Atelier Carvalho Bernau typeface, http://carvalho-bernau.com

GobQ volunteers: Qualified candidates please send résumé to our P.O. Box [GobQ. LLC, PO Box 11346, Portland, OR 97211] or to gobq@yahoo.com

Special thanks to Craig Florence, Michael Heald, Rhonda Hughes, Kevin Sampsell, & Curtis Whitecarrol

Copyright © 2013, by Gobshite Quarterly, GobQ LLC., Individual Contrib. Copyrights notwithstanding...

All rights reserved & tra la la & boo-fucking-hoo....

Respectfully flip the book over, as Issue 14, Spring 2014, is a whole upsy-daisy 48 pgs away fr. the centre

Gob Words A word to give offense, when offense may be due. ***Gobshite***, per OED, is what the American crew of Adm. Perry's Expedition to Japan were called by the natives; American Heritage Dictionary, 4th. ed., refers to a wad of expectorated chaw & to the Old Eng. *Shiten*; yet another dictionary refers to a Gobshite as a "*pernicious blatherskite*"—in other words, a stiff to read the teleprompter feed for CNN or for Rupert Murdoch's Fox "*News*" bullshit mountain. & these are the people offended by the word, so think before giving in to those who'd control speech (& by ext., thought). Indeed, why else are censors so vigorously censorious? Is this good or bad? Wasn't it Pulitzer who said that journalism should comfort the afflicted & afflict the comfortable? Quick, is this good or bad? (...& it hurts to have to ask, as this went to press in late fall, 2013, but... Has the federal government shut down *again*?) (Good or Bad?) One of our goals is to present the best writing fr. around the world, w/ works orig. published in another language presented *en face*. Quick, is this good or bad? & who decides? Quick... — ***rvb***

The Usual Suspects
Contributors

Anonymous, history's most prolific author (when not engaged in on-line insurgencies, returns w/ *The Coming of the Fire Wyrm*, an 18th. C. Icelandic pome, trans. by Michael Lohr.

Tomislav Marijan Bilosnić is a Croatian writer & painter. A prize-winning poet, who's also written several novels & essay colls. He makes his *GobQ* debut w/ 2 *en face*

pomes (fr. the coll. *Wrought Silver*).

Julienne Bušić, a writer & translator, has been published in UK, US, Bosnia-Herzegovina, & Croatia, where she's resided since 1992. Her memoir (of revolution, plane-hijacking & prison), *Lovers & Madmen*, was published in the UK, translated into Croatian, won a 1996 award, & is the basis of a recent documentary. A freq. *GobQ* contrib., Bušić returns w/ a short story, about an American childhood.

Dan Cross is an Australian comic book writer, collab. here w/ M. Fikaris on *Endless Karma: First World Problems.*

Trevor Dodge, member of Spanbauer's Dangerous Writing workshop, has work in journals incl. *Hobart*, *Golden Handcuffs Rev.*, *Gargoyle*, & *Fiction International*. He has a new coll., *The Laws of Average*. *Literacy* is his *GobQ* debut.

Kathrine Dunn, survivor of Portland's Reed College & several yrs of exile in Ireland & other European locales, has worked day-, & night-, jobs've incl. house painting, bartending, voice-over work, teaching creative writing at Lewis & Clark College, writing for Willamette Week, & hosting a KBOO FM literary radio show. Her noves incl. *Attic*, *Truck*, & *Geek Love*, the last a modern classic. Other projs. incl. *Death Scenes: A Homicide Detective's Scrapbook*

(1995), a photography book for which she wrote the text. Dunn is a contrib. & ed. for *cyberboxingzone. com,&* her writing on boxing, widely reprinted, has won awards; her concise, trenchant & biting memoir, *What it Means*, is a BestGob reprise fr. GobQ #12.

Dan Encarnacion co-curates Portland, OR's Verse In Person poetry series. His pubs incl. *MARGIE*, Berkeley *Rev.*, *&/or*, *Eleven Eleven*, *SPLIT*, *& Exquisite Corpse*. *I Consider Myself Healthy* is his *GobQ* debut.

Michael Fikaris is an Australian comic book artist, here collab. w/ D. Cross on *Endless Karma: First World Problems*.

Peter H. Fogtdal, who divides his time betw. Copenhagen & Portland, has written 12 novels in Danish. *The Tsar's Dwarf*, here extracted *en face*, is his 1st. novel published in English, by Portland's Hawthorne Books.

David Hapgood, a Portland-based journalist, makes his *GobQ* debut w/ *Every Edge A Centre: Chinguetti (Mauritania)*.

Roman Karlović, a Croatian writer & translator, makes his GobQ debut w/ *en face* translations of Tomislav Marijan Bilosnić pomes.

Filip Kavala, born in Zagreb, 1977, has had his comics in *Endem & Bruh*, & other Croatian comic strip mags. He divides his energies between comics & architecture.

Helena Klačocar-Vusksić, raised in Bosnia, is a founding member of the Zagreb artistic group ZZOT; her works incl. an award-winning graphic novel based on her yr at sea; excerpts from *Dittmamman*, & fr. *Strip Tattoo, are incl. in this issue*.

Covadonga G. Lahera, a Madrid-based critic, has work in *Transit*, *cine y otros desvíos* (a Spanish online cinema journal), as well as other pubs. *Holy Motors: Who We Were When We Were*, is her *GobQ* debut.

Michael Lohr returns to *GobQ* w/ a translation of Anonymous's Icelandic pomes.

M. F. McAuliffe, a founding *GobQ* ed., w/ work in journals incl. *Overland, In Other Words: Merida, , Adelaide Rev.*, & *Gobshite Quarterly*, returns w/ 2 essays.

Adrian Martin currently teaches in Germany, & writes var. pubs. His *Holy Motors: Who We Were When We Were* translation is his *GobQ* debut.

Ярослав Могутин / **Slava Mogutin**, a NYC-based Russian poet, journalist, & artist, wrote for glastnost indie Russian pubs as a teenager; by the age of 21, he'd gained critical acclaim & official censure for his journalism & queer art. Targeted in 2 high-profile criminal cases, Mogutin got US political asylum, via PEN & Amnesty International; in fact, a forthcoming collection, *Food Chain*, due Mar., 2014 fr. ITNA Press, includes those writing that drove Slava fr. Russia, & would land him in prison under Putin's new laws. Slava's art & writing are in pubs. incl. *Village Voice*, *i-D*, Vice, *El Pais*, *L'Uomo Vogue*, & *BUTT*. His pome *Paris Belly*, incl. along w/ a photograph fr. his portfolio, is his *en-face GobQ* debut.

Tiina Nunnally, a US translator of over 40 Scandinavian books, is excerpted here w/ *The Tsar's Dwarf*, en-face.

Daniele Pantano is a Swiss writer & translator, whose own writings, & Georg Trakl translations, are in journals incl. *Absinthe: New European Writing*, *Guernica Mag.*, *Jacket*. Pantano's most recent books incl. *In an Abandoned Room: Selected Poems by Georg Trakl*.

Domi J. Shoemaker self-identifies as an Idaho-raised Portland-steeped, gender-fucker. A member of Spanbauer's Dangerous Writing workshop, & host of the quarterly Burnt Tongues readings, her job experiences incl.: youth advocate, intake & crisis intervention specialist, & collab. art bandit w/ Lidia Yuknavitch. Domi's work is in *Unshod Quills*, & *[PANK] Online*. *A Fish* is Domi's *GobQ* debut.

Georg Trakl (1887 – 1914) began writing at the age of 13. In 1912, Trakl's pome *Vorstadt im Föhn*, & all his subsequent work, was published in Innsbruck's *Der Brenner*. In 1913, Trakl's *Der jüngste Tag* appeared. During W.W. I, Trakl volunteered for service, & served on the Eastern Front as a medical officer, in Grodek, in Galicia. He died (allegedly OD'd) following a nervous breakdown in 1914.

Graham Willoughby, whose artwork has adorned our covers since the 2nd. issue, returns, w/ simpler, starker, but no less evocative covers for the Spr. 2014 issue, as well as for the Winter 2014 issue on the other side. Graham has exhibited in US, German, Spanish galleries, & his native Australia. He's published several artist books in Australia, & in the US, w/ Rochester's Visual Studies Workshop Press; many are in museum & library colls. worldwide. Q

Zagreb, Hrvatska / Croatia

Portfolio / Alkohol Ubija, graphic novel, Filip Kevala

HEIMS NARÐAN

Frá móðurkviði jarðar rís ég
skreiðandi skuggi Miðgarðs Ormsins
inn í þoku meinfýsinar nætur,
ég geng samhliða myrkrinu og klæðist hornum styrksins,
vegna þess að ég er sá sem ét hið dauða
hin mikilfenglegi ormur.

Gnýr hins ódauðlega dreka
söngl rísandi leðju nornarinar,
móðir sortinar jarðar,
ég er eld narðan.

Innra með mér býr óttinn sem finna má á tunglslausum haust nóttum,
skelfing sú sem dynur á kvíðafullum stríðsmönnum Týs,
því að meðan sólin sest og tunglið fyllist
sést þar brennandi höggormur koma niður fjallið
sál þín nötrar.

Gnýr hins ódauðlega dreka
söngl rísandi leðju nornarinar,
móðir sortinnar jarðar,
ég er eld narðan,
rísandi frá sköpum Skálda.

Og ég er það sem klífur regluna.
— *Anon.*

COMING OF THE FIRE WYRM

From the womb of earth I rise,
slithering shadows of the Midgard Serpent,
into the mists of the most malevolent of nights,
I walk among the darkness and wear the horns of power,
for I am the eater of souls,
the great fire wyrm.

Roar of the immortal dragon,
chant of the mud witch rising,
mother of the blackened earth,
I am the serpent of fire.

With me resides the fear found on moonless autumn nights,
those terrors that awash the warriors of Tyr in dread,
for as the sun sets and the moon comes on full,
watch the burning serpent descend from the mountain,
and feel your soul shiver.

Roar of the immortal dragon,
chant of the mud witch rising,
mother of the blackened earth,
I am the serpent of fire,
rising from the Womb of Skaldi.

And I am the schism in the order.
— *trans., Michael Lohr*

España

HOLY MOTORS: ¿CUÁNDO ÉRAMOS QUIENES ÉRAMOS?

Claro que hemos sido muchos. Y llegará probablemente el día, y más de uno, en que nos preguntemos quiénes carajos somos, o fuimos, si el final biológico está cerca. Como en una ingenua e in extremis tentativa de poner orden al asunto de la propia existencia, o simplemente por querer jugar a un último juego, asumiendo la imposibilidad de la victoria, que te quedarás a medias o fracasarás, y aceptando la propia confusión y el irremediable desorden de las cosas. O viceversa. Pero jugar pese a todo.

Justo arrancando Holy Motors me creía en una reversión del inicio de Fellini 8 y ½, en algo así o dentro de alguna otra consciencia en plena voluntad retrospectiva, pero no identificaba a ningún clon atascado en un embotellamiento subjetivo, y también se me cruzaban Zelig con algún Bergman y Los ojos sin rostro. Tampoco no significa que no fuera un sueño. O una equivocación.

Y una indigestión de pluridentidad empieza a cobrar forma, en la pantalla y en el patio de butacas: esto era un actor veterano (tanto de mentira como de verdad), para algunos casi un familiar, cuyo trabajo consiste en disfrazarse hasta once veces al día, o más. Y en cada uno de esos disfraces se deja un pedazo de vida y en los más exigentes, toda

Spain

HOLY MOTORS: WHO WE WERE WHEN WE WERE

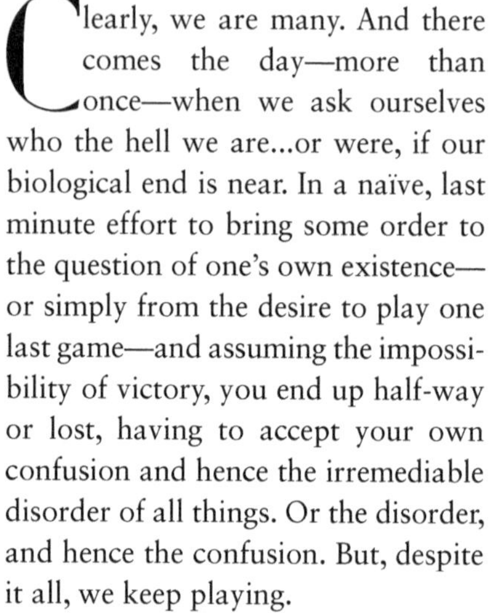

Clearly, we are many. And there comes the day—more than once—when we ask ourselves who the hell we are...or were, if our biological end is near. In a naïve, last minute effort to bring some order to the question of one's own existence—or simply from the desire to play one last game—and assuming the impossibility of victory, you end up half-way or lost, having to accept your own confusion and hence the irremediable disorder of all things. Or the disorder, and hence the confusion. But, despite it all, we keep playing.

At the very beginning of *Holy Motors*, I thought I was watching a reversal of the start of Fellini's *8½* (1963); I was inside something of that sort, some other consciousness in full, retrospective flight. But I wasn't just identifying with this clone caught in a subjective traffic jam; I also recalled a mixture of *Zelig* (1983), a few Bergmans, and *Les yeux sans visage*. But nothing indicates that it wasn't all a dream. Or just a mistake.

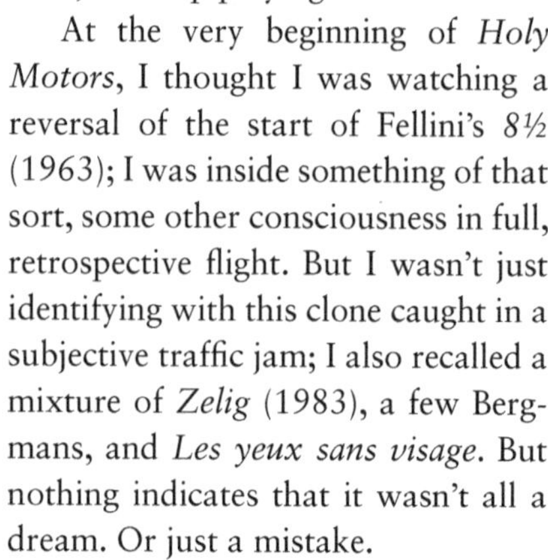

So, an overload of multiple identities begins to take shape, on the screen and in the stalls: this man, Oscar/Lavant, is a veteran actort (as much in the film as in real life), for some virtually a family member, whose job is to don a costume maybe eleven times (or more) a day. And in each of these roles, he leaves behind a piece of his

la barra de energía. Casi siempre se pone al borde de algún abismo y no se confunde porque es un actor enorme y cuenta con una estupenda chófer (Edith Scob, también veterana de la pantalla) y una pautada agenda, y un envidiable armario de ropa y complementos en el asiento trasero. Las bambalinas van dentro de una limusina y de allí puede salir el mundo entero. Y se abre una puerta como asciende el telón. A veces, desgastado, el imponente actor desea la muerte de todos los papeles. La Muerte.

Hay también una mujer que no pudo ser y la resurrección de un personaje anterior al grito de "mierda" y una erección que se duerme. Pero en realidad nada de esto fue, pues también eran mentira la hija, la mujer, el asesinato del político, la mendiga, el prehistórico hombre verde, la motion capture y aquella carrera-simulacro sobre una cinta de gimnasio (¿qué habría hecho Muybridge con ella?) durante la que podría haber sonado el "Modern Love" de Bowie. Y todas las lágrimas falsas, sobre todo todas las lágrimas. Y, sin embargo, seguimos pagando entradas, solicitando acreditaciones, aguardando tiempos de descarga, accionando plays. Salimos del cine dentro del cine, y del cine dentro del cine, despojados, desnudos, recién nacidos, y decidimos volver a la limusina.

Y de pronto sí, tanto tiempo llevaba dormido tras nosotros que despertó, el tísico de Carax empijamado entre cuatro paredes y dis-

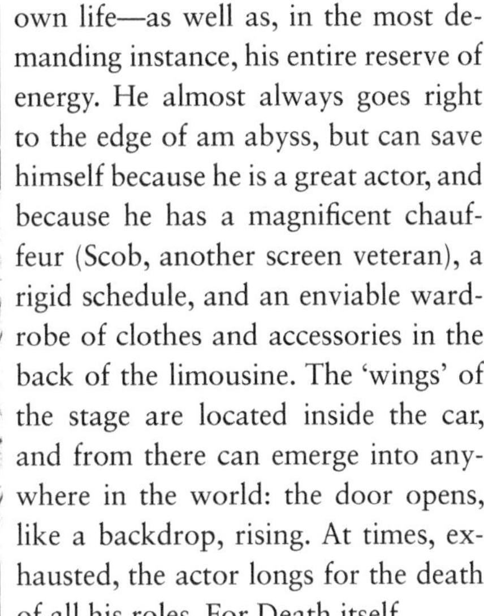

own life—as well as, in the most demanding instance, his entire reserve of energy. He almost always goes right to the edge of am abyss, but can save himself because he is a great actor, and because he has a magnificent chauffeur (Scob, another screen veteran), a rigid schedule, and an enviable wardrobe of clothes and accessories in the back of the limousine. The 'wings' of the stage are located inside the car, and from there can emerge into anywhere in the world: the door opens, like a backdrop, rising. At times, exhausted, the actor longs for the death of all his roles. For Death itself.

There is also a woman who was never meant to be (Kylie [Minogue]); the return character who embodies the cry of 'merde!'; and an erection that falls asleep. But, in reality none of this ever existed; likewise, we can categorise as lies the deceitful daughter, the politician's murder, the beggar, the prehistoric green man, the Motion Capture, and that simulated-run on a gym treadmill (what could Muybridge have done with that?)—during which Bowies 'Modern Love' might have played. And all the phony tears—especially the tears. But we keep bying tickets, requesting critics' accreditations, looking out for download windows, and hitting 'play', We exit the cinema inside the cinema, then we go to the cinema outside that cinema—and then, stripped naked like a newborn babe, we decide to return to the limousine.

And suddenly, yes, after so long sleeping behind us, he finally wakes up: the consumptive, pajama-wear-

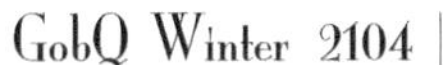

puesto a romper una sala. Sale de la tumba de su dormitorio y nos pone frente a nosotros mismos: público que mira a público. Quizá solo quede ya esta imagen inquietante; o quizá es la única imagen que existió siempre, conteniendo todas las demás. Los espectadores frente a los espectadores, recibiendo la última visita, encajando la última bala anunciada para nosotros. El otro día se la llevaba el triste Álex Mala sangre. Y tantos años después aquel director sonado regresa de entre los muertos, casi, para invocar a través del cine su propia resurrección, representando una última función arrebatada, reapropiándose una vez más de un cuerpo llamado Denis Lavant, una invasión por quinta vez, una invasión múltiple con múltiples máscaras y múltiples lugares, mucho más profunda.

Por primera vez Lavant no se llama Álex sino Óscar ‡, y el director que mezcla sus letras deja su viejo nombre y se renueva con su segundo, y entonces aquella vieja extensión anatómica de la nueva ola, aquel viejo fantasma de intermitente enfant terrible vuelve a retorcerse y travestirse para festejar con la boca abierta una valiente, sonora e irónica carcajada donde se reúnen todas las historias vividas y las que quedaron por vivir, las contadas y las que quedaron por contar, y la autonomía de una autoría orgullosa en su desmesura y en la de su propio actor gigante, ambos dispuestos a morir en cada

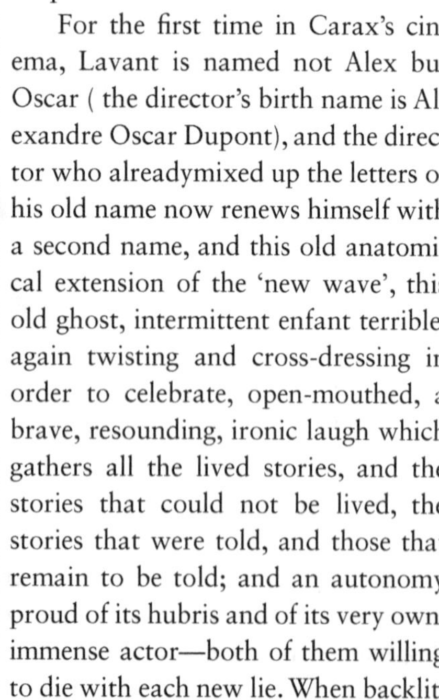

ing Mr. Carax himself, caught between four walls, and willing to break through one of them. Free of his bedroom-tomb, Carax confronts us with ourselves: one audience views another. Perhaps only at this moment is the image disturbing; or perhaps it is the only image that has ever existed, containing all the others. Spectators before spectators, receiving the ultimate visitation, taking the final bullet with our name on it. Once upon a time, that was sad Alex and his 'bad blood'. And now, so many years on, this crazy director returns, almost from the dead, to invoke, through cinema, his own ressurection: representing a final, vehement performance, reappropriating, once again, that body named Denis Lavant, invading it for the fifth time—a multiple invasion—with multiple masks and multiple locations, far deeper than ever before.

For the first time in Carax's cinema, Lavant is named not Alex but Oscar (the director's birth name is Alexandre Oscar Dupont), and the director who alreadymixed up the letters of his old name now renews himself with a second name, and this old anatomical extension of the 'new wave', this old ghost, intermittent enfant terrible, again twisting and cross-dressing in order to celebrate, open-mouthed, a brave, resounding, ironic laugh which gathers all the lived stories, and the stories that could not be lived, the stories that were told, and those that remain to be told; and an autonomy proud of its hubris and of its very own, immense actor—both of them willing to die with each new lie. When backlit, mentira. A contraluz una limusina puede parecer un coche fúnebre. Y viceversa.

— *Covadonga G. Lahera*

25 oct., 2012, en Esbozos, Portada, Transit, cine y otros desvíos

‡) Léos Carax es un anagrama resultante de su primer y segundo nombre de nacimiento, Alexandre Oscar Dupont. Denis Lavant ha sido dirigido por Carax en cuatro largometrajes (más el segmento "Merde" de la irregular Tokyo!, 2008): Chico conoce chica (Boy Meets Girl, 1984), Mala sangre (Mauvais sang, 1986), Los amantes del Pont Neuf (Les amants du Pont-Neuf, 1991) y Holy Motors (2012). En los tres primeros el protagonista se llama Álex. En este último, sin embargo, el personaje al que interpreta Lavant se llama por vez primera Óscar.

a linousine may seem like a hearse. And vice versa.

— *trans., Adrian Martin*

(orig. in *Transit, cine y otros desvíos, Oct. 2012*)

IPRC

1001 SE Division St
Portland, Oregon
97202 USA

Open Hrs.

Mon: 12noon - 10pm
Tue/Wed/Thu: 4pm - 10pm
Fri: 12noon - 10pm
Sat: 12noon - 6pm
Sun: 12noon - 5pm (youth only)
Sun: 5pm - 10pm (all ages)

Contact Us or Visit!

Dec. Classes & Workshops include

1 & 8 Dec. Crazy Cartooning Class for Youth (noon)
8 Dec. Pen to Print: Your Stories (3 PM)

(503) 827-0249 | info@iprc.org | http://www.iprc.org

I CONSIDER MYSELF HEALTHY

The sun is weaning itself from warming our yawning morning risings. It seems to want me to wake from heat from you. A change in gravitational pull would destroy our green world, could bring life to Mars. The Roman god of war and a candy bar. The violent evolution of civilization or nutty pleasure for your tongue. They both satisfy desires that we have determined to be opposed to a heroic life. I consider myself healthy. The sun is weaning away our warm yawning morning risings—seems to want m e t o w a k e f r o m h e a t f r o m y o u.

— *Dan Encarnacion*

"a stark, riveting theatrical experience"
– The Oregonian

Portland Experimental Theatre Ensemble
presents
Song of the Dodo

November 9 – 24
Thurs. – Sun., 8 PM
Studio 2, 810 SE Belmont, Portland, OR

December 3
7:30 PM
Tom Miles Theatre, Pacific University, Forest Grove, OR
Box Office: (503) 352-2918

tickets & info: www.petensemble.org

tickets & info: www.petensemble.org

"a stark, riveting theatrical experience"
– The Oregonian

Portland Experimental Theatre Ensemble
presents
Song of the Dodo

November 9 – 24
Thurs. – Sun., 8 PM
Studio 2, 810 SE Belmont, Portland, OR

December 3
7:30 PM
Tom Miles Theatre, Pacific University, Forest Grove, OR
Box Office: (503) 352-2918

Zagreb, Hrvatska / Croatia

Three Words & the Universe

Julienne Bušić

The girl heard the Mother come in and tried to hold back her jagged sobs, stuffing a corner of the blanket in her mouth, pulling the pillow over her head to muffle the sound. It was unrealistic to expect the Mother not to hear, and she should have known better, but the longing that had overwhelmed her, a yearning she could not name, was not to be contained.

Honey, what's the matter, why are you crying? said the Mother as she lifted the pillow from the girl's head. The girl became suddenly silent, stopped breathing, forced her limbs to freeze in place, as though she had just died. Hoping she would turn to ice and melt and then the Mother would have nobody to ask and then she would be left to her sorrow.

Honey, what on earth is the matter? The Mother tried to gently extract the corner of blanket from the girl's mouth, but her jaw had also frozen in place, and the blanket had become a permanent though somewhat soggy appendage.

She tried to block the sound of the Mother's voice from her tiny part of the universe, tried to transcend the bed, the room, the house, the starry sky, to go to him, to go to Roy Rogers, King of the Cowboys, symbol of all that was good and fine, moral and brave. Roy would be on Trigger, his golden, ageless palomino. Oh, that gorgeous creature, she thought in ecstasy as her mother's voice faded. Trigger's platinum mane and tail blew gently in the breeze that came off the mountains, the Rocky Mountains, she believed, or maybe the Grand Canyon. Roy wore his traditional red kerchief tied snugly around his neck. His eyes were slits, in a Chinese sort of way, though Roy Rogers was an all-around American, 100%, of that she was sure. His equitation was perfect, the hands lay relaxed on the withers, the reins loose but not too loose. Trigger could shy unexpectedly—a bird exploding from a tumbleweed; a prairie dog emerging from its hole with a squeal—and if the reins were too loose, Trigger could rear up or buck and Roy could take a pratfall, end up on the ground in shame. With his hat askew, his kerchief wadded up like an old washcloth. Not Roy Rogers. The reins were loose, but would never be too loose.

Dale Evans was there, too, Roy's wife, even though her name wasn't Rogers. The girl had often wondered how that could be possible, but preferred it that way, since to her that meant a certain distance, a lack of intimacy between them which gave her great comfort. Dale was on her smaller Buckskin, Buttermilk. Trigger and Buttermilk were almost as famous in the United States as Roy and Dale, especially among those who preferred animals to people. The girl vacillated on that issue, depending upon the events of any given day.

Some hypothesized about the relations between Trigger and Buttermilk. They made a handsome pair, the golden stud and the golden mare. And of course they were always together so it would have been convenient in the event there were any chemistry between them. But the girl's focus was not on the horses, it was on Roy Rogers. Roy, Roy Roy Roy. Sometimes she would repeat the name a hundred times in a row, to herself and then out loud, until it became sort of like a prayer or a secret incantation which would then transport her into a higher realm that made her feel weak at the knees, as though they were attached to her legs by rubber bands, not actual bones or tendons.

Roy Roy Roy. She would gaze at him several times every day, from the pages of this or that movie star magazine. Piles of them lay stacked under her bed, each with a story about Roy, about the colors he liked and favorite foods. His cowboy hat was always so clean and white and she had often wondered how he managed to keep it that way, considering all the dust out on the prairie. It never got bent out of shape and was never cockeyed, but always perched there on his head at the perfect angle. He always wore plaid shirts, sometimes a blue print, sometimes red, long-sleeved and tucked neatly into his blue jeans. The jeans fit his form perfectly, not too baggy, not too tight, and the contours of his thigh muscles were just perceptible underneath, while his calf muscles were obscured by the cowboy boots, which went up to just under the knee. His boots were hand-tooled and custom made to fit his feet. The toe and heel tips were silver and the actual boot black lizard with fancy stitching all over it.

Stitching that curled around and then Honey open your eyes it would be partially hidden by the stirrups and she felt her shoulder being shaken.

Honey, wake up, you're having a bad dream!

She opened her eyes slowly and looked at her mother with deep loathing. You just ruined my world, she said so that only she could hear.

She continued to stare at her mother, as though in a trance. Not blinking, not even once. The corner of blanket lay soggy on her arm.

Everything's OK. It was only a dream, said the Mother in a singsong way, as though reciting a nursery rhyme. Eeny meeny miney moe.

She continued to stare hollowly.

Why were you crying, honey, do you remember? Did you want something?

Yes. She wanted Roy Rogers. Wanted to meet him, see him, be with, be him. But she could not put it into words, not even for herself, and certainly not for her mother. Realizing she would have to say something so that her mother would leave, she opened her mouth and whispered the first thing that came to mind: A cowgirl outfit.

Her mother laughed in a conspiratorial sort of way.

"Oh, a cowgirl outfit? Well, you know your birthday's in a few days, so you might just get your wish. Now back to sleep, it's the middle of the night!" Her mother tucked her in and quietly left the room.

The girl tried to get back to Roy. That was all she wanted, Roy, Roy Roy Roy Roooooy. When she said his name out loud instead of just thinking it, the R would began deep within her, starting in the pit of her stomach and working its way up, through the lungs, when it was overtaken by the O as her mouth opened, and then into the throat, the Y, finally coming out like a wail as her mouth position changed again to accommodate the final letter.

A cowgirl outfit! She shook her head in disgust.

* * *

She had invited five guests to her birthday party, three girls and two boys, all of whom sat squirming around the kitchen table with idiotic, shiny pointed hats perched on their heads. There was Pam, and Jeanie, and Jeri. And Fred and Tom. They had already devoured the chocolate cake and ice cream, and had played pin the tail on the donkey (they had let her win on purpose, and she, following the unwritten rules for hosts and hostesses, demurred and proclaimed Fred the winner).

Now it was time to open the presents. It was the usual unimaginative collection: a plastic jewelry set, a bead making kit, a box of pastel water colors, a diary, and a pair of slipper-socks with bunnies on the toes. The gift from her parents was the last one remaining. She narrowed her eyes, hands in her lap, just looking at the box.

Honey, open your last present, said the Mother. It's from mom and dad!

She reached for it with one hand, hooked her little finger around the ribbon and pulled it to her, as though it were infected.

The guests all leaned toward the present in anticipation, eyes wide, palms flat on the tabletop.

She ripped off the ribbon, tore the paper ferociously with both hands, as though trying to dig herself out of the loose dirt of a living grave, and opened the box. Inside was a cowgirl outfit, a two-piece suit, jacket and skirt, red, with white plastic fringe along the arms and at the bottom of the skirt.

Oooooh, sighed the girls. The boys snickered.

Try it on in your room, honey, and then come out and show your guests! said the Mother.

She went in her room and crawled underneath the bed. When her mother came in, she was with Roy, with Trigger, Dale, and Buttermilk. Her cowgirl suit was in a wrinkled ball in the corner of the room.

I feel sick, she told the Mother from under the bed. Everyone better go home.

The mother left, taking one last sad look at the cowgirl outfit, closing the door quietly.

* * *

They were one of the first on their block to get a television. The Father had brought it home one day after work, set it up on what they called a TV table in the living room, right in front of the couch with the big, plush arms. Now she would finally be able to watch the Roy Rogers show, see Roy in person as it were, how he moved, his acts of bravery, kindness, generosity. Watch him gallop across the prairie, through the mountains. All she had seen so far were his pictures in the movie star magazines, the mute, unmoving, and one-dimensional Roy, fixed in time and space, in perfection.

She checked the newspapers. The Roy Rogers Show wasn't on until Thursday, two days to wait. She sighed. But there was another cowboy movie coming up, "The Left-Handed Gun," about Billy the Kid, with the actor Paul Newman as Billy. She had heard of him, vaguely. His eyes, she knew, were very blue. She might as well watch, and that meant she needed to make her preparations.

First she went to her bedroom and got two belts. Then she returned to the living room, buckled them together to fashion makeshift stirrups, hung them over the arm of the couch, got up onto it, and adjusted them to the right length for her feet. Then she got back down and took another two belts, buckled them together as well, and looped them around the front of the arm to serve as reins. When this was done, she turned on the television, climbed back onto the arm of the couch, took the reins in her hands, put her feet into the stirrups, and waited for "The Left-Handed Gun" to begin.

Her younger brother Stewart came in and tried to change the channel to "Mister Moon." She threatened to tickle him till he wet his pants, so he gave up and lay down in front of the television in his traditional position on his back, arms underneath his neck, legs bent at the knee, feet pointing back toward his head. It was this flexibility that had been decisive in his winning all the local twist championships with the neighbor girl, Chrisanne.

Like Billy the Kid, the girl was left-handed, too, and proud of being different than the majority of the world's population. She and Billy, and who knows what other famous people were left-handed. Some said left-handed people were crazy, or possessed. Which was probably the reason the girl down the street, Susan, wasn't allowed to play with her. She sat on her makeshift horse and watched the movie develop. The horses were the first thing she noticed, and she would immediately decide which she preferred at the very beginning. The one with the white stripe down its face, or the two white stockings, or the small pinto. Maybe the palomino, because it reminded her of Trigger. She could only guess at the intensity of the colors since everything was black and white.

But as soon as Billy the Kid made his first appearance, she forgot about everything else, the horses, Pat Garrett, the Mexican women with their ebony hair and eyes and low-cut dresses and skirts that swirled around like boomerangs. She even forgot about Roy, who had suddenly become a paper doll, speechless and expendable from the safe refuge of a movie magazine under her bed. She felt herself becoming very light in the saddle, as though part of her had floated out toward Billy, leaving her as insubstantial as a sigh.

Billy being taught to read the Bible by the kindly Englishman, who was gentle and loving. Explaining to him the meaning of seeing something "through a glass darkly." And Billy suddenly comprehending a deep and profound truth. His hair, how it curled around his ears, moist and darker now from the light sweat which had broken out on his temple. And then warning the Englishman not to go out alone on the prairie, without a gun. Shortly thereafter the sound of gunshots. His dead body being thrown over Billy's horse.

"But Billy, you hardly knew him" said one of his fellow cowpunchers when Billy vowed revenge on the guilty parties.

Billy had looked up and out—with eyes transparent and full-out, out to nowhere, except it was somewhere, it was his heart, his soul. "I knew him," he moaned, with the accent placed equally on all three words. She tightened her reins, pulled them in close to her chest. The way he said it, it was as though he had become the man, had taken into himself the Englishman's death and pain, the injustice. There was nothing more to say, even if he had wanted to.

The perfection of that phrase. The way he had made it represent everything that had happened, everything he felt, his love for the Englishman, his agony at his death, the need for revenge, the knowledge, the passion.

With those three words he had achieved perfect unity with the universe. She jumped off the couch, the stirrups sliding to the rug. Her brother looked up in surprise, having been engrossed in Billy's next move. She flung open the front door and ran outside. Her feet were barely touching the ground, her feet burned, everything burned, her chest, her loins. It felt as though her hair were on fire, ablaze, sparks shooting up toward the sky in waves.

"Ahhhhhh," she screeched as she began to circle the house. "Ahhhhhh......"

She ran and ran, lap after lap after lap after lap, her arms flailing at her sides, legs circling like bicycle wheels. The love, and the knowledge of it, Billy's need to destroy, to explain, the eyes, so clear and full, with ruined cities and lives behind them...those three words.... She ran and ran, passed the hedge and thought "bush", which led her on to another and another word, nothing quite capturing the essence. And the cloud hanging over the Greenberg's house, shaped like a pigtail, or maybe a lasso just after the knot's been undone, hanging free, or maybe... Her face was flushed and sweat was running in rivers down her face, nose, chin, and still she ran and ran, and with each step, she began to understand why she had said it, why she had said "cowgirl suit" to the Mother when she had meant Roy, and then understood that if she had said Roy, it still wouldn't have been enough, because she meant it all, all of it, everything at once. And she'd never be able to say it, because one thing always led to another, out into eternity. She took one final lap before collapsing on her back in exhaustion, eyes directed toward the heavens. Q

Little Beirut, Oregon

Literacy

Trevor Dodge

"Bipolar depression is proof there's no God. Well, at least proof that there's no New Testament God. Old Testament God, now, that's a different story. He probably cooked that shit himself. Like meth."

He swizzled the plastic stick around in his glass. The ice cubes got out of the way.

"And frankly I don't know who's worse for marriage, the homos or the crazies. I was reading the other day how 90% of marriages with a bipolar person end in divorce."

Seems too low, I said. Sounds like bullshit, I said. Where did you read that? I said.

"Don't remember. Does that make a difference?"

Difference in what, I said. Difference in it being true? I said.

"No, difference in where I read it. I know that ain't true."

That's what I'm getting at, I said. But you know it ain't true, I said. That seems connected to where you read it, don't you think? I said.

"Not really. Not anymore. Everybody's always reading all kinds of bullshit from all kinds of bullshit places."

Fuckin' literacy, I said.

"Damn straight."

We clinked glasses because he had his raised. I don't never leave a bro' hanging. Q

ENDLESS KARMA FIRST WORLD PROBLEMS
HUZZAH!
WHAT UP?
:BEEEP:
-I JUST WON A YEARS SUPPLY OF PENS!
SO, THAT'S EQUAL TO LIKE... FIVE PENS?... THEY WILL PROBABLY SEND YOU 5 PENS
WAY TO KILL MY BONER MAN...
the NEXT DAY.
HEY, WAKE UP MAN-THERE'S A PACKAGE HERE FOR YA'
JUST THREE PENS! ASSHOLES!! SUCH A BIG BOX TOO...
-FUCK THIS! I'M GOING BACK TO BED MAN!!
ENDLESS KARMA IS WRITTEN BY DAN CROSS & DRAWN BY MICHAEL FIKARIS
endless-karma.tumblr.com

"This collection accumulates the power, skill, passion, and intelligence of his poetry to the point where I wonder, is anybody writing better than this?"

— Ursula K. LeGuin, *poet, novelist, & essayist, author of Hard Words, Earthsea Trilogy, & Lavinia*

A WHITE CONCRETE DAY:

POEMS: 1978 – 2013

DOUGLAS SPANGLE

Published September, 2013, by

REPROBATE / GOBQ BOOKS

ISBN 978-1-62847-660-6 $19.95

A limited edition of 15 signed numbered copies is available @ $34.95 each

order on-line @

http://www.gobshitequarterly.com

also available at Mother Foucault's Books, Broadway Books, Powell's Books, & St John's Books

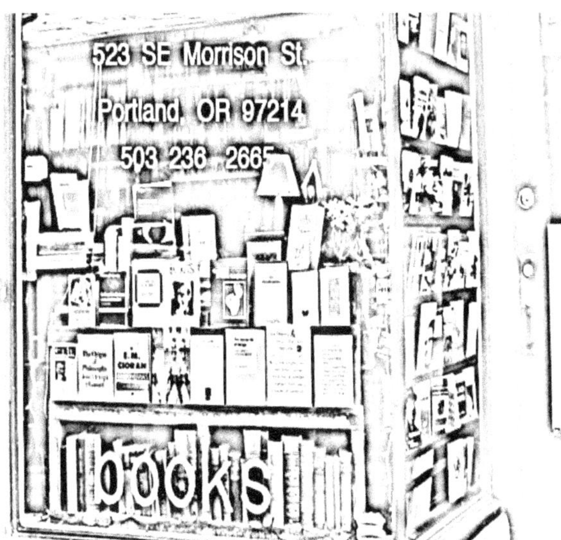

IN DER HEIMAT

Resedenduft durchs kranke Fenster irrt;
Ein alter Platz, Kastanien Schwarz und wüst.
Das Dach durchbricht ein goldener Strahl und fließt
Auf die Geschwister traumhaft und verwirrt.

Im Spülicht treibt Verfallnes, leise girt
Der Föhn im braunen Gärtchen; sehr still genießt
Ihr Gold die Sonnenblume und zerfließt.
Durch blaue Luft der Ruf der Wache klirrt.

Resedenduft. Die mauern dämmern kahl.
Der Schwester Schlaf ist schwer. Der Nachtwind wühlt
In ihrem Haar, das mondner Glanz umspült.

Der Katze Schatten gleitet blau und schmal
Vom morschen Dach, das nahes Unheil säumt,
Die Kerzenflamme, die sich purpurn bäumt.

— Georg Trakl

IN THE HOMELAND

Scent of mignonettes strays through the sick window;
An old square, chestnuts black and wasted.
A golden ray breaks through the roof and flows
Onto the siblings, dreamlike and confused.

Decayed things float in the slop, the föhn wind
Coos softly in the small brown garden; very quietly
The sunflower enjoys its gold and melts away.
The watchman's cry rings through blue air.

Scent of mignonettes. Bare walls grow dark.
The sister's sleep is heavy. The night wind delves
Through her hair bathed by lunar glow.

The cat's shadow glides blue and slender
From the rotten roof hemmed by coming misery,
The purple rearing of a candle's flame.

— *trans., Daniele Pantano*

DIE BAUERN

Vorm Fenster tönendes Grün und Rot.
Im schwarzverräucherten, niederen Saal
Sitzen die Knechte und Mägde beim Mahl;
Und sie schenken den Wein und sie brechen das Brot.

Im tiefen Schweigen der Mittagszeit
Fällt bisweilen ein karges Wort.
Die Äcker flimmern in einem fort
Und der Himmel bleiern und weit.

Fratzenhaft flackert im Herd die Glut
Und ein Schwarm von Fliegen summt.
Die Mägde lauschen blöd und verstummt
Und ihre Schläfen hämmert das Blut.

Und manchmal treffen sich Blicke voll Gier,
Wenn tierischer Dunst die Stube durchweht.
Eintönig spricht ein Knecht das Gebet
Und ein Hahn kräht unter der Tür.

Und wieder ins Feld. Ein Grauen packt
Sie oft im tosenden Ährengebraus
Und klirrend schwingen ein und aus
Die Sensen geisterhaft im Takt.

— *Georg Trakl*

THE PEASANTS

Ringing green and red before the window.
In the low, smoke-blackened hall
Farmhands and maids have begun their meal;
And they pour the wine and break the bread.

From time to time a scant word drops
In the deep silence of noon.
The fields shimmer without end
And the sky leaden and vast.

In the stove a hideous glow of embers
And a swarm of flies buzzes.
The maids listen, dumb and mute
And blood pounds in their temples.

And sometimes lustful glances meet
When animal fumes waft through the room.
A farmhand intones the prayer
And a cock crows beneath the door.

And back to the field. Horror often
Seizes them in the raging roar of wheat
And with shrills the scythes swing
Ghostly back and forth in time.

— *trans., Daniele Pantano*

Чрево Парижа

Весна и Фаллос на работе
отдал свой вкус морской пехоте
ты приходил незваным гостем
что было странно при твоём-то росте
не верь себе
как я тебе не верю
я закрываю глаза
и ты выплываешь оранжевым

нежным и ласковым зверем
приоткрывая тебе и твоим дружкам двери
я пытаюсь втереться в доверье

я боюсь подойти к телевизору
из него появляется ХУЙ РАЗМЕРОМ С ЭКРАН а
ещё я боюсь машинистов подъЁБного крана

ты забываешь слова
но они вспоминаются снова
для обозначения этой болезни
существует специальное слово

я путаю имена
мои случайные связи
не доведут до добра и меня
уже вряд ли спасут специальные мази

я опять открываю двери
не дай бог с тобой оказаться в чреве
парижа
НУ ЖЕ!
НИЖЕ!

— *Ярослав Могутин*

Россия / Russia

PARIS BELLY

It's Spring
            and a hard-working Phallus
left its taste for sailors' might
You came as an unexpected guest
strange for your kind of height

Don't believe yourself
just like I don't believe you
I close my eyes and you swim out orange
a delicate tender beast
Openning doors for you and your fellows
I'm trying to rub against your trust

I'm scared to death to approach the TV set
out comes this screen-sized cock full of scream
I'm also scared of COCKstruction workers
their cream

I forgot some words
but they come forwards
There's a special term
to signify this illness
I get names mixed up
My accidental associations
Won't lead to kindness
and special oils won't provide consolation

I again open the doors
God forbid to find myself with you
in Paris Belly
Come on
Get down on me
GET DOWN!

—Transl., Slava Mogutin

A Fish

Domi J. Shoemaker

Coming out of the Tunnel after switching is so much different than going in before. The first time I was aware of coming back out, it scared the hell out of me. I already hated being in the hospital and had told myself I didn't belong there. All that changed when Harley had taken over and I didn't get to say a damn thing about it.

After the fish hatchery trip we all came back to the hospital. I waited until the 4 pm med call to give Peaches that little whirling fish. Med call is a good time for passing off contraband because most of the staff are attending to the loonies lined up at the med window, to make sure they haven't cheeked or passed off their meds.

I told Peaches to line up first, and then meet me in the bathroom after she took her meds. She showed up like I asked, and I took her into one of the stalls, so she could see the fishy, and we could then ditch the evidence. The damn thing had been stuffed in that cigarette pack in my bra for over ran hour, and it stank.

In a move that would make me either a friend or an asshole depending on the outcome, I started the flush, then pulled the cigarette pack out of my bra, and dumped Whirling Fish in.

"Look Peaches," I said. "Fishy is swimming."

Real slow, Peaches' thin, thin lips, stretched wider and wider across her dentures. When she smiled, her eyes squooshed half shut. One Pepto Bismol pink slipper got to tap tap tapping dogscratch quick on the honeycomb tile floor. Then she raised her bony hands to pat the top of her silvery braided hair. I had to wind it down before Peaches exploded.

"Yep, that's your fishy," I said. "She came for a visit, now we gotta send her back home."

Peaches' bones got to shaking, and she set that Pepto Bismol Pink housecoat to twirling, yelling, "Fishy fishy. Jonni fishy."

Though I tried to stop her, Peaches ran out of the bathroom still yelling. "Fishy fishy, Jonni fishy."

I stashed the box in the Kotex dispenser and ran after her. By the time I got to the day room, some of the other loons chimed in. I couldn't see Peaches, her being so short, but judging by the commotion in the TV corner, I figured that's where she was.

I was halfway across the room when I heard a whoop and a holler. Out of the group busted Barbie, heading straight for me.

"Fishy fishy, Jonni fishy." Barbie yelled, stripping off her pajama top and stringing it between her legs.

Last time I'd seen Barbie, she had on her own tie-dyed hippie dress, so she was wearing that and a floppy leather hat when she was discharged. I hadn't been there but a few days, but she was real shy and sweet. She flashed me a peace sign when they let her out the door. Rumor had it that Barbie used to lived on an old school bus. Seven or eight times charged with arson, never competent to stand trial. Seven or eight times before the County finally went to check on her to make sure she took her meds and didn't blow herself up. That time, they found her bus in Southern Idaho. She was way out in the desert covered in tinfoil, so they didn't find her.

Now here she was, her hair bleached blonde, and ratted up in front, bangs at least 6 inches high, sky blue eye shadow. No mascara. Mascara brushes qualify as weapons. Hospital Pajama bottoms and a bra, riding her pajama top like a bucking mule. Bright red lipstick.

"I've got a fishy for you, Jonni," Barbie said.

I had to get to Peaches.

Next thing I know all hell broke loose.

Five, ten, hell, I don't know how many dancing around hollering, "Fishy fishy, Jonni fishy."

There were whoops and hollers every few seconds as interns and orderlies wrangled loonies who had no intention of being wrangled.

I finally saw Peaches, and it was all I could do to try to separate her from the group so she didn't get blamed for all that mess.

Peaches was twirling.

"Fishy, Jonni, Fishy."

I spun her around behind my back. I would take the blame.

It was my fault. I'd just tell them that I was telling Peaches about the fish hatchery trip and she got all excited.

But Fucking French Fry got there first. What the fuck was his angle?

He must have figured out that Peaches had started the chant and I saw him writing in his stupid little notebook. Probably that Peaches "upset the milieu."

I stepped up to French Fry and put my arms out front, all go-ahead-arrest-me-like.

"It's all my fault," I said. " I was just trying to..."

Just as I'd stepped up to take responsibility for my actions, like I've been told to do all my life, the motherfucker interrupted me.

"Nice try, Jonni," French Fry said.

"No, really. It's my fault." I was telling the truth, but French Fry knocked right through me, right into my shoulder, to get to Peaches.

I don't know why they had it in for Peaches and I was sick of them picking on her. Any time something happened they went for the smallest and weakest one least able to defend herself. Hell, she didn't have a god damn person outside that place who gave a shit about her.

I tried to stop him. "Come on guys, leave her alone. It was all my fault."

Peaches kept whirling and kept chanting while they restrained her.

"Fishy fishy, Jonni fishy."

I can't tell you what I don't know; I can only tell you what I remembered next.

I knew I wasn't in the dayroom anymore, but I was not sure where I was. I drifted somewhere between pitch black nothing, and the memory of being tucked down into that one old sweat-stained canvas sleeping bag, that great uncle's mildewed sleeping bag. Maybe my grandpa's old moldy canvas tent.

Yes, grandpa's old canvas tent. I am seven years old again and camping with Grandpa. The safest place in the world.

I am happy and safe with cream-colored long-johns bunched up under my blue flannel nightgown.

I couldn't hold on to any thought long enough to pull it off. Filthy ashtray taste. Mouth so dry I couldn't swallow. I started to panic.

My heart skipped and double-beat a few times. I tried one last time, pulled the sleeping bag over my head. No sleeping bag, no flannel nightgown. Just my Levi's and the smell of canvas strong enough that it stayed on my tongue and mixed with ashtray when I opened my mouth to suck in a breath. And Harley was the only one who smoked. I wasn't seven anymore.

A small popping and buzzing, soft light filtered through my eyelids. I fucking hated pink. Puffy-eyed and struggling to focus, I had to stretch my eyebrows up and wrench my jawbone down just to pry my eyes open enough to see a pair of gray canvas sneakers a few inches away from my face.

I was on my side, on the floor. I tried to push myself up, but the arm I was laying on just lay there tingling. My other arm burned with lactic acid so I dropped it back down. My energy was zapped. I turned my eyes to the floor. Linoleum. Green linoleum squares that used to fit together, to look seamless, now calked with grime.

I closed my eyes and recited the script from the Mind Is Body Is Mind group. Cognitive Behavioral Training.

Breathe In through the nose and into the belly. Trip the vagus nerve.

Calm fight or flight. Breathe in. Vagus. Breathe Out.

Regain control of muscles. Breathe in, breathe out, and try not to puke.

Now open your eyes, I said to myself.

Brown corduroys and shoes. The shoes uncrossed and crossed again. I knew those shoes, that corduroy. Fucking French Fry. I didn't want to talk to that son of a bitch until I knew what I wanted to say.

I rolled onto my back to release the arm that was numb underneath me. It still tingled, but at least I could move it.

"You about done, Jonni?"

"Your sneakers are filthy." My voice came out rough, and deeper than usual.

I sat up. The cold linoleum was harder beneath my ass than it was beneath the fatty cush of my tummy and boobs.

"Little nap after your workout?"

My periphery was restored.

French Fry was sitting backwards on the weight bench tapping his No.2 pencil on the empty heavy bag stand next to him.

Nap? Workout?

The exercise room was an old patient room, cleared out and repopulated with a universal weight machine, two stationary bikes, and my favorite, the heavy bag. If you played their game, you'd earn enough privileges to work out alone for up to an hour. Alone as in sight and sound supervision... Staff could use cameras with audio to supervise. If you were a perfect little voluntary like me, they must not pay attention at all because the heavy bag was knocked off the stand, and I'd been using it as a pillow.

There were benefits to being there because you wanted to be there.

"These fucking lights."

I closed my eyes again for a moment.

French Fry got up and stepped past me to the keyed light switch beside the door.

A click of his key and the overhead fluorescents buzzed and popped back off. I opened my eyes. The vertical seam of the heavy bag was ripped and a hand full of cotton batting poked through. I flexed my right hand. Stiff and sore.

"I gotta lock up," French Fry said. "Snack Time."

Fuck Snack Time. A fucking joke. Peaches barely does anything and gets strapped to a gurney in seclusion. As far as they knew, I lost my shit, and beat the hell out of a heavy bag until they offer me snacks.

"You really went to town." French Fry laughed. "Way to use your coping skills."

I pulled a tuft of cotton batting out of the heavy bag, balled it up, then dropped it on the floor.

"Coping skills." I said.

"If you show me that last move, I'll erase the video of your workout."

He knew I had no idea what move he was talking about and I was pretty sure he had no access to the surveillance system.

"Fuck you," I said. "Asshole." *Q*

Fc2

www.uapress.ua.edu

ISBN: 978-1-57366-171-3 / $18.95 Paper

ISBN: 978-1-57366-839-2 / $18.95 EBook

The juice is well worth the squeeze.

— Tony McMillan, digboston . com

Kaasten Alonso fracks the mother tongue.

—Michael Martone, author of Four For a Quarter

Portfolio / Fingered, photography, Ярослав Могутин / Slava Mogutin

Ярослав Могутин / *Slava Mogutin has forthcoming exhibitions in Berlin, Paris, Prague, & Amsterdam, fr. Dec. 2013 through Feb., 2014*

Every Edge A Centre: Chinguetti

David Hapgood

The ancient part of Chinguetti was built mainly of dry stone architecture — rocks stacked without mortar — and the alleys between the buildings were slowly filling in with sand: the dunes were in the process of consuming the town. We passed several doorways that were already buried almost to the top. In any case, the place was nearly deserted. At its center was the minaret of Chinguetti's mosque, a square tower consisting of thirty feet of stacked orange and brown rocks, topped at each corner by ostrich eggs on sticks: fertility symbols. This mosque was one of the oldest on earth and was a national symbol of Mauritania. But the sand that had drifted into the alleys around the mosque had raised the vantage points, making the minaret appear much shorter than it actually was.

Just as I was getting used to the idea that the old quarter was essentially a ghost town a man in a crisp white desert robe and indigo turban came around the bend.

"Are you looking for the library?" he asked.

"Sure," I replied, after an awkward pause. I knew that the ancient libraries of Chinguetti had been renowned throughout the western regions of the Sahara many centuries ago, back when the oasis had been a center of religious learning and a crossroads on the caravan trails. It was our good luck that we had run into this librarian, as it was an opportunity to forget about what had happened back at the auberge.

He led us to a building made of stacked rock, just like the others except the excess sand had been carted away from its doorstop. The facade was entirely without ornamentation, apart from triangular shaped air vents made of rock, incorporated into the wall. The man took out a large old key with a wooden handle and metal brush-like lobes at the end, and demonstrated how it worked in the old lock. Then he insisted that I give it a try. After that he invited us inside the building.

The library's interior consisted of little more than a dark room with stacked rock walls, a palm beam roof and a sand floor. But it was filled with hundreds of large, ancient books, piled high on a long table, down on the floor, on a mud ledge in the back, and on several metal shelving units, the only concession to modernity in the building. There was no electricity, and it was so dark inside that we had to keep the door open.

In medieval times, students had traveled long distances on pilgrimage to Chinguetti's many schools and libraries and had gone on as scholars, poets and jurists to spread the good word about Chinguetti all the way across the Sahara, and beyond: the town's name was well known as far away as the Arabian peninsula. This is what had earned this remote place its former reputation as one of the so-called Great Cities of Islam.

The librarian placed several large manuscripts on the table and opened them: first a Quran and then the 'Hadith' — the teachings of The Prophet. Each page was hand inscribed, and even the less ornate examples were masterpieces of Arabic calligraphy. He went on to show us books with pages made of gazelle skin, and then paper manuscripts that had been damaged by termites.

"We will restore these," he said, and then showed us a book he had recently mended.

Enormous stacks of parchment lay everywhere in the shadows, books that had escaped their bindings. I couldn't tell where one volume ended and another began: how he would ever put it all in order? It would take a hundred years.

"You are from America?" he finally asked.

"Yes," I replied.

"We only get three or four Americans a year."

He took out the library guest book and leafed through it until he found an entry of interest.

"Look," he said, "The American ambassador. He visited six months ago."

Sure enough, there it was.

I told him that I worked in a library back in America, and this seemed to please him — we were kin, of a distant sort. Q

Knitting Alone For Thousands of Miles: Arundhati Roy Speaks of Our Fridge

M. F. McAuliffe

The fridge died sometime Sunday afternoon. Stuff in the freezer was melting. There was no running sound.

This had happened several times over the life of this particular fridge. It was 8 years old when it died on January 15.

The life-span of a refrigerator used to be between 20 and 30 years. (Remember The Secret Life of Machines?)

We had to throw out anything that might have been damaged wholly or partially by defrosting or de-cooling. Between $200 and $400 dollars' worth of groceries. Between one and two thirds of a week's net income for the household. This had happened at least twice a year for 8 years, and after the 3rd year Amana refused to reimburse us for the losses.

We emptied the freezer first.

Frozen tacos, chicken-legs, ice-cream, ice-cream bonbons (from my birthday the night before); buffalo burgers, chicken legs, frozen sections of Italian loaves and French baguettes (for toasting later); the ice-packs for strains & muscular treatments.

Then the fridge. Half and half, non-dairy hazelnut vanilla, butter, olives, artichoke hearts, salami, brie, cheddar jack, pancetta, bread, English muffins, corn tortillas, flour tortillas; tomato sauce, Worcestershire sauce, chili sauce, vinaigrette, balsamic vinegar; peanut butter, almond butter, cranberry spread, pumpkin butter spread. As the contents went down the sink or into the Green Bin feed I almost began to cry.

Greek olives, Italian salami and pancetta — all that work, growing them pickling them pimento-ing them transporting them, unpacking them stocking them storing them — all those ships across all those seas, all those trucks across all those mountains, along all those valleys — all that history and effort. The whole world was going down that drain.

The Amana: $1600. Around two weeks' gross income for the household. The new Frigidaire: $1500. Around two weeks' gross income for the household.

Between them a month's gross income. This year we will donate a twelfth of our income to large corporations for products which have already proven to be a waste and laying waste of time, energy, steel, oil; of planetary resources and the lives of everyone who made and moved them. And the new fridge may quite possibly prove to be the same.

In order to go on producing this shiny

rubbish, oppressive factories are being built in China, warlords are running slave-mines in Africa.

The answer to the question — whether corporations will permit any mindset but their own to survive — trembles on a razor edge, the outcome of the adivati resistance movement in the adivati forests of India.

There, gigantic mines have been planned and promised to gigantic companies. The mining-rights have been sold out from under the original inhabitants. The adivati are fighting to not be dispossessed, made landless, homeless, destitute, fugitive, reduced to trying to survive between the edges of the processes that are turning the whole planet to glossy crap.

Our kitchens depend on this kind of war. Our lives do. Q

Walking with the Comrades, Arundhati Roy, Penguin Books, NY/London/Mumbai, 2012

HOTEL DE
PS

PUBLICATION STUDIO MEXICO D. F.

PUBLICATION STUDIO

books made fresh daily

www.publicationstudio.biz
ps@publicationstudio.biz
717 SW Ankeny Street
Portland, Oregon 97205

Mon-Fri: 11am-5pm

717

Colón PARIS ROMA

What It Means...

Katherine Dunn

The brothers said it, joking or pissed, in easy talk or intense argument. When the mothers said it there was trouble. You get invisible fast to escape the wave of scorched air sweeping the kitchen.

It was usually a short sound as hard as a fist in the face. But it had many other forms and uses. It could be drawn out into broken syllables as in fu-uh-uhk! With a sharp bite at the end for dismay or rage. It could stretch on a long lilt of breath for amazement. It could be linked with animals or relatives, body parts or machinery.

Mr. Grease at the gas station made it a poem as he sweated under the hood of a gasping Chevy on a hundred degree day chanting, "Fuck the fuckity fuckin' fucker." Hearing his music stunned me with delight. It became my private song, never uttered in company, a whispered incantation of the most powerful of all words. Later, when the teacher tried to teach the parts of speech and the forms of a sentence, the chant became my secret model. Verb, noun, adjective, adverb — act, object and modifiers — all in this one magnificently dangerous word.

However it was voiced, whatever tune or tension carried it, I had no notion what it meant. Something extremely bad, because the brothers got their heads rapped with spoons or thimbles or spatulas if they said it in front of the mothers, and the mothers said it so rarely and only when they were hurling thunderbolts. Still, precisely what it was I didn't know.

Then one sleepy summer afternoon I was perched high in the maple tree out front when the new girl from down the street came boldly into our yard and climbed up beside me without an invitation. I'd watched her family move in but had never seen her up close. She was caramel colored, tawny skin, hair and eyes. I don't remember how our conversation began but before long she was asking me if I knew what "fuck" meant. I shook my head, mute at having this taboo territory broached.

"My brother told me," she said. "It's when a guy gets mad at his wife and kills her and lays her out flat on the floor in the back bedroom. Then her brother finds out and kills the husband and lays him out right on top of her. And then the husband's sister finds out and kills the brother and puts him right on top of the husband. And then the husband's father kills the sister and lays her on top and her mother finds out and kills him and lays him on top, and all the relatives kill all the relatives and lay them one on one, up and up, until the whole room is filled with stacks of dead bodies. That's what it means — "fuck you."

The dreadful weight of this explanation was so true to the power of the word as I heard it, that I believed it completely. The puny definitions that came to me later were uninteresting by comparison. Q

GRAD

Ako me pogleda i ja ću vrisnuti,
ako me još jednom zaprozori ova prljava i gola zgradurina.
Mala kuća i velika kuća,
bez prigovora na beton i aluminij,
a ovaj što navodno ima mnogo zdravlja samo je staklo.
Ni stara drveta, ni mrtva lista, ni zgažene travke,
samo neon bez ruku, samo neon s bijelim siromaštvom.
Doći će dakle noć i ništa se neće promijeniti,
okolo toga sve prazno puno, ni neba, ni zemlje,
samo ljudska trupla kao naplavine
i svemir strahovitih stijena.

— Tomislav Marijan Bilosnić

TIGRICA ČEKA TIGRA

Samo se jednoj tigrici
takve stvari događaju
U današnje vrijeme
samo jedna tigrica čeka tigra
Cijeli svijet iščekuje
što će se dogoditi
hoće li ga dočekati
Nešto slično zbilo se vrlo daleko
i vrlo vrlo davno
nitko više ne zna što se zbilo
Je li tigar poginuo
od oštrog noža
ili je tigrica ostala živjeti
s kraljem čuvajući mu sina
Davno, vrlo davno
sve što je bilo čudno događalo se
pa nitko više i ne vjeruje
da tigrica danas čeka tigra
da će joj prije srce prepući
nego što će se umoriti od čekanja

— Tomislav Marijan Bilosnić

Zagreb, Hrvatska / Croatia

THE CITY

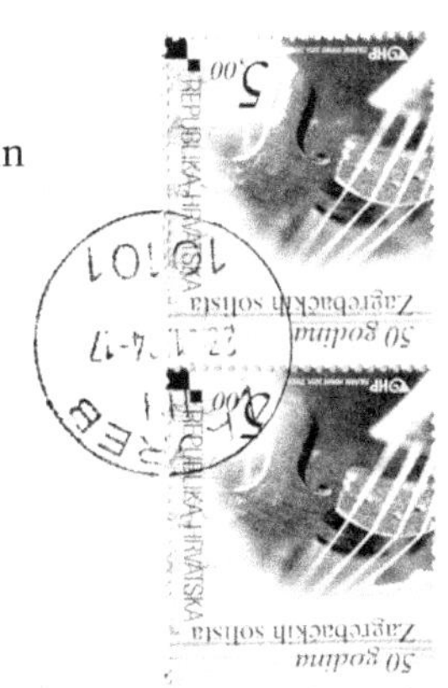

If it glares at me, I'm going to scream—
should this huge building, bare and filthy, bottle me in
A small house, a big house,
no complaining about the concrete and aluminum,
and the one that's supposedly healthy is all glass.
No old trees, no dead leaves, no trodden grass,
just armless neon—just neon and white poverty.
So night will fall and nothing will change.
The environs are all voidly full, no sky, no earth,
just human corpses like silt,
and a universe of frightening rocks.

— *Transl., Roman Karlović*

A TIGRESS WAITING FOR THE TIGER

This can happen
to just one tigress
These days
just one tigress is waiting for a tiger
The whole world is anxious to see
what will happen
will he eventually arrive
Something like that happened far, far away
and a long, long time ago
no one knows what happened any more
Was the tiger killed
with a sharp knife
or did the tigress live on
with the king, tending his son
A long, long time ago
all kinds of strange things happened
so no one believes any more
that the tigress is still waiting for the tiger
that her heart will rather break
than weary of waiting

— *Transl., Roman Karlović*

Pred Zavjesama

Prijatno mi je ovako samom u maloj sobici podkrovlja.
To je jedino još sigurno.
Uključit ću tv - portabl,
zapaliti poklonjenu cigaretu John Player Special
i razmišljati o otplati knjiga moje biblioteke.
Pred zavjesama sam, spustit ću ih,
ne želim kroz prozor gledati svijet.

Ako je jutro proživjet ću još jedan dan!
Ako je podne vraćam se sigurnom zaklonu noći!
Ako je večer napit ću se kao autokradica!
Ako je noć izgubit ću vrijeme u svinjarijama!
Liječim društvenu bolest bombardiranjem mira
I želio bih snove o vinogradima,
ali snovi neće pomoći.

Da mi je osjetiti udarac kopite po glavi.
Zatvorio bih oči i mislio jasno,
dok građani spavaju mirno.
Uopće neme ničega, samo bivaš stariji za dan
i ponekad sanjaš da te neće pozvati iza zavjesa.

— Tomislav Marijan Bilosnić

Before the Curtains

I like being alone like this, in my tiny attic room.
That's the only certainty left.
I'm going to turn on my portable TV,
light the John Player Special cigarette they gave me,
and find some way to pay off the books
I keep on my shelves.
I stand before the curtains. I'll draw them down—
I refuse to look out of the window at the world.

Morning come, I'll live through another day.
At noon, I'll head back to night's safe sanctuary.
I'll get drunk like a car thief in the evening.
I'll waste my time in abominations in the night.
Bombing the peace is a form of social therapy for me,
and I'd love to dream of vineyards,
but dreams won't do.

Would that I felt a hoof hit me on the head!
I'd close my eyes and clear my thoughts,
while the community had sweet dreams.
Nothing is there, nothing at all,
you just grow a day older
and dream, every once in a while,
you won't be summoned behind the curtains.

— *Transl., Roman Karlović*

Portfolio / Ditmamman, Helena Klačocar-Vusksić

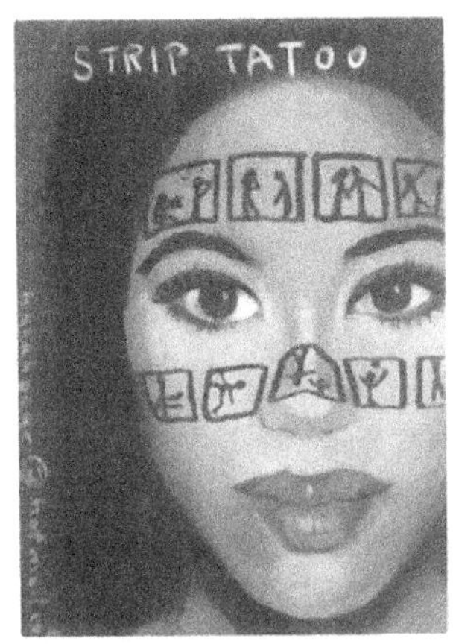

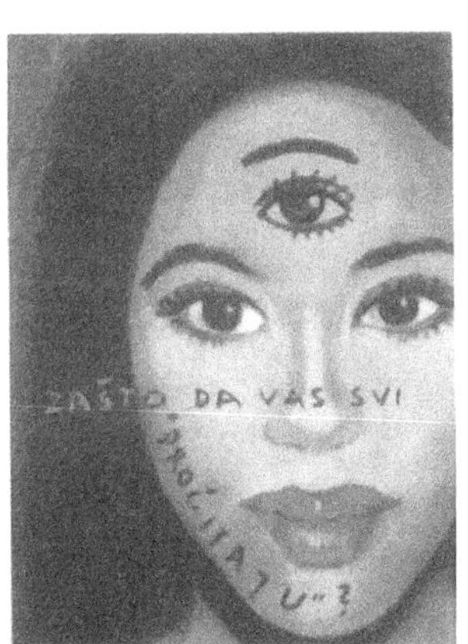

Portfolio / Strip Tattoo, Helena Klačocar-Vusksić

Danmark / Denmark

Fra Zarens Dværg

Peter H. Fogtdal

Måske er det enfoldigt, men jeg venter på Zaren. Han må snart komme for at besøge mig, ellers var jeg ikke blevet bragt her.

Men han viser sig aldrig.

Måske har Zaren for travlt med at føre krig, regere landet og bygge kanaler i hans hollandske paradis. Jeg ved blot, at jeg savner Peter Aleksejevitj; at han en dag vil hente sin danske dværg, og så vil min fremtid være sikret. Så kan jeg flytte ind i hans palads, være vredladen på den måde, jeg kan være vredladen på og håne dem, der skal hånes.

Men alt, jeg får lov til at være, er en saltstøtte.

Jeg skal stå på min plads i Kunstkammeret, se ud i luften uden at møde de fines blikke. Hvis de spørger mig om noget, skal jeg svare, ellers skal jeg holde min kæft. Hvis de kaster med penge, må jeg godt samle dem op. Hvis de befamler mig, skal jeg sprede, hvad der er nødvendigt at sprede.

Nogle dage får jeg kun en kiks og et bæger brændevin. Vi har tigget om at få tæpper ned i stalden, men efter at hermafroditten er stukket af, er vores kår forringet. Hvor han/hun er flygtet hen, ved vi ikke. Vi bliver forhørt om

From The Tsar's Dwarf

Peter H. Fogtdal
trans.,
Tiina Nunnally

Maybe I'm being naïve, but I'm waiting for the tsar. Surely he will come soon to visit me; otherwise I wouldn't have been brought here.

But he never makes an appearance.

Maybe the tsar is too busy waging war, governing the country, and building canals in his Dutch-inspired paradise. All I know is that I miss Peter Alexeyevich, and that one day he will come for his Danish dwarf, and then my future will be secure.

Then I'll move into his palace, and I'll be hot-tempered the way I'm often hot-tempered, and I'll mock those who deserve to be mocked.

But the only thing I'm allowed to become is a pillar of salt.

I have to stand at my station in the Curiosity Cabinet and stare straight ahead without meeting the eyes of the fine folk. If they ask me something, I'm supposed to answer. Otherwise I'm supposed to keep my mouth shut. If they throw money at me, I'm allowed to pick it up. If they grope me, I'm supposed to spread whatever it's necessary to spread.

For several days I get only a cracker to eat along with a goblet of vodka. We've begged for a few blankets down

sagen, men ingen ved noget. Frederik Ruysch er rasende. Hermafroditter er dyre; det er ikke let at finde en ny på dagens marked. Ruysch skriver rundt til raritetskabinetterne i Dresden, Hanover og Paris og prøver at bytte med en haleneger, men ingen er interesseret. Noget tid senere finder man den gamle hermafrodit død i en datsja, øjensynlig ved selvmord.

Nikolaj Zigant har været væk fra Kunstkammeret et halvt år. Han har fungeret som Zarens vinkyper på en rejse til Sortehavet. Peter Aleksejevitj elsker franskmanden, der er et hoved højere end ham selv. Men en dag kommer Nikolaj tilbage. Hans kår bliver ikke forbedret. Han skal stadig stå nøgen i de iskolde lokaler.

Nogle gange sniger jeg mig ind for at kigge på ham.

Nikolaj er et rigtigt mandfolk; det kan en gammel kælling som jeg godt lide. Jeg stirrer ofte på hans saftige pik og betragter hvordan den hænger mellem benene som en knippel.

En dag forelsker Nikolaj sig i en af de kvinder, han tvinges til at befrugte. Hun er finsk og næsten lige så høj som ham selv. De er et mageløst par; de kan ikke stå oprejst noget sted i verden; de må kravle ind ad døre og sidde på taburetter, der braser sammen som korthuse. Når de går ture i haven, skraber de hovedet mod himlen. De er perfekte, men får ingen børn. I et år står de side om side i Kunstkammeret, hånd i hånd, nøgne som Adam og Eva – Zarens tårnhøje yndlinge.

in the stable, but after the hermaphrodite ran away, our circumstances have gotten worse. I have no idea where it has fled. We're questioned about the matter, but no one knows a thing. Frederik Ruysch is furious. Hermaphrodites are expensive, and it's not easy to find another in today's market. He writes to various curiosity cabinets in Dresden, Hanover, and Paris, attempting to trade a monkey man for a hermaphrodite, but no one is interested. Sometime later the old hermaphrodite is found dead in a dacha, apparently a suicide.

Nikolai Zhigant has been away from the Curiosity Cabinet for six months. He has been serving as the tsar's wine steward during a trip to the Black Sea. Peter Alexeyevich loves the Frenchman, who is a head taller than he is. But one day Nicolai is back. His situation has not improved. He still has to stand naked in those ice-cold rooms.

Several times I sneak in to have a look at him.

Nicolai is a real man. That's something that an old hag like me can appreciate. I often stare at his juicy cock, observing how it hangs like a truncheon between his legs.

Then one day Nikolai falls in love with one of the women that he's been forced to impregnate. She's a Finn and almost as tall as he is. They're a marvelous couple. They can't stand upright anywhere in the world. They have to crawl through doorways.

They sit on stools that collapse like a house of cards.

Zaren har mange yndlinge.

Jeg er glad for, at jeg ikke er en af dem.

Hvorfor er jeg ikke blevet lykkeligere af at kende Gud?

Jeg havde fred i sjælen, da jeg boede i klosteret. Jeg fandt en mening med lidelserne, men i det jeg kom til byen, åd verden sig ind på mig. Det tog mig mindre end en dag at lære, at intet har ændret sig. Jeg var tilbage, hvor jeg altid har været: dybt begravet i Guds skarnbunke.

Jeg er rasende.

Jeg er altid rasende.

Måske er raseriet det eneste, der giver mening?

Måske er raseriet Gud?

Jeg vågner to år senere rystende af kulde.

Der er rimfrost på høet. Peterborgs sne står ind gennem brædderne, borer sig under huden og fremelsker forkølelser. Alle dårligdomme drypper fra himlen – den himmel, jeg tilbad i klosteret, hvor jeg fandt ro og tillid i intetheden.

Zaren kom endelig forbi for nogle måneder siden.

Han hilste på mig, kyssede på munden og hastede videre. Jeg er ikke sikker på, han huskede sin danske dværg. Jeg er ikke sikker på noget som helst: Hvor længe jeg har været her; hvor ofte jeg har vist mig frem for folk og fæ.

Måske har jeg stået i Kunstkammeret, siden jeg blev født.

Frederik Ruysch eksperimenterer på mig. Han tager mit blod, stikker mig med nåle og studerer mine ekskrementer.

When they take a walk in the garden, they scrape their heads against the sky. They're perfect together, but they don't produce any children. For a year they stand side by side in the Curiosity Cabinet, hand in hand, naked as Adam and Eve. The tsar's towering favorites.

The tsar has many favorites.

I'm glad that I'm not one of them.

Why don't I feel any happier after finding God?

I felt a peace in my soul while I lived in the cloister. I found a purpose behind my sufferings. But when I returned to the city, the world ate its way into me. It took less than a day to learn that nothing had changed. I was back where I've always been: buried deep in God's garbage heap.

I'm furious. I'm always furious. Maybe fury is the only thing that has meaning. Maybe fury is God.

Two years later I wake up shaking with cold.

There is frost on the straw. Petersburg's snow is coming through the slats of the wall, boring its way under our skin and coaxing out wretched colds. All manner of misery drips down from the sky — the sky that I worshipped in the cloister, where I found peace and a faith in nothingness.

The tsar finally paid a visit a few months ago.

He greeted me, kissed me on the lips, and hurried onward. I'm not sure that he remembered his Danish dwarf. I'm not sure about anything at all. How long have I been here? How often have I been

Han måler min korte hals med sin passer, skraber en stor luns af en finger og lægger den på en tallerken. Jeg skriger rædselsslagent, men Ruysch hører mig ikke. Han beretter, at dværge var skattede i oldtidens Egypten. Det kan man se i flere udgravninger i ørkenen.

Ruyschs ansigt er jovialt og koncentreret, mens han mishandler mig. Mine skrig generer ham ikke. Da han er færdig, lukker han sig inde i sit kontor med sin Bibel og mine tal. En dag bekendtgør han, at jeg rent faktisk har en sjæl.

– Hvorfor tror I det? Har I fundet den i Jeres mikroskop?

Ruysch kigger på mig med et godmodigt smil.

– Sjælen er usynlig, Surinka.

Jeg protesterer:

– Hvis den er usynlig, kan I jo ikke se den.

– Du har menneskelige træk. Dine deformiteter skyldes din mors angst under graviditeten. Du er ikke et monster, du kommer ikke fra Djævlen. Du er Guds skabning.

– Det er jeg ked af at høre.

– Hvorfor det?

– Jeg vil gerne komme fra Djævlen. Det ville give mig et formål.

– Er der ikke noget formål i at komme fra Gud?

Jeg sukker og får øje på et spejl. Mit hår er gråt, kinderne er indfaldne. Jeg har stadig ikke nogen hals.

– Vi er glade for at have dig her, siger Frederik Ruysch med pludselig varme.

– Hvorfor det? spørger jeg forbavset.

– Fordi du er rap i replikken.

– Kan man kun være rap i replikken,

put on display before man and beast?

Maybe I've stood in the Curiosity Cabinet since the day I was born.

Frederik Ruysch is experimenting with me. He takes my blood, sticks me with needles, and studies my excrement. He measures my short neck with his calipers, scrapes a big slice of skin off my finger and puts it on an oval plate. I scream in terror, but Ruysch doesn't hear me. He's not interested in my screams.

Instead he tells me that dwarves were once treasured in ancient Egypt. We were treated like gods. He knows this from what they've found inside the pyramids and from the excavations in the desert.

Ruysch wears an amicable expression as he manhandles me. He's always talking about an Egyptian god named Bes, the god of sexuality and childbirth, but I have a hard time listening to him. When Ruysch is done with his examinations, he locks himself in his office, where he studies both the Bible and my numbers.

One day Ruysch admits that I actually do have a soul.

"Why do you think so?" I ask dryly. "Did you find it under your microscope?"

"The soul is invisible, Surinka."

Ruysch gives me a good-natured smile.

I object. "If it's invisible, then you can't see it."

" You have human features. Your deformities were caused by your mother's fear during pregnancy. You are not a monster.

You are not from the Devil. You are God's creature."

"I'm sorry to hear that."

"Why is that?"

"I would prefer to come from the Devil. That would give me a purpose."

hvis man har en sjæl?

Frederik Ruysch ler. I et kort øjeblik tror jeg, at han vil omfavne mig, men så rækker han ud efter nogle papirer. Jeg betragter hans sære ansigt, der falder sammen, når han kigger ned. Hvor gammel er hollænderen mon? Halvfjerds år, firs? Og hvad er det, der får ham til at behandle os så ilde? Er det glæden ved at ydmyge de miserable og de elendige? Er han et menneske, som andre frygter – som nyder at gøre ondt for at hævde sig selv? Faktisk virker det ikke sådan. Frederik Ruysch leder blot efter sandheden. Ruysch er en forsker, der vil forstå verden, koste hvad det vil. Han vil opstille regler og love for alt. Hvor andre ser kærlighed, ser han matematik.

Mit blik glider ned til hans adamsæble. Den gamle mand er ikke god til at barbere sig.

Da jeg er tilbage på min plads, længes jeg tilbage til dengang, jeg ikke havde nogen sjæl. Q

"Is there no purpose in coming from God?"

I pause to think about his question.

Frederik Ruysch laughs. For a moment I think he's going to hug me, but then he reaches out for some papers. I look at his strange face that collapses whenever he looks down. I wonder how old the Dutchman is. Seventy? Eighty? And what is it that makes him treat us so badly? Is it the joy of humiliating those who are wretched and miserable? Is he a person that other people fear? The kind who enjoys inflicting pain in order to assert himself? That doesn't really seem to be the case. Frederik Ruysch is simply searching for the truth. Ruysch is a scientist who wants to understand the world, no matter what the cost. He wants to institute rules and laws for everything. Where others see love, he sees only mathematics.

My eyes slide over his Adam's apple, which always has a few stray hairs on it. The old man isn't very adept at shaving.

When I'm back at my station, I long for the time when I didn't have a soul. Q

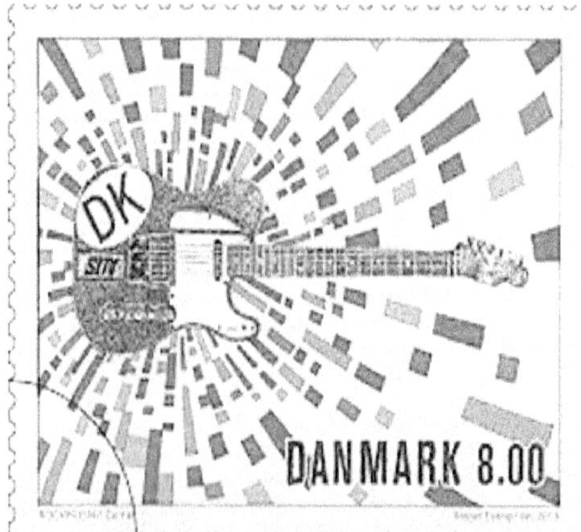

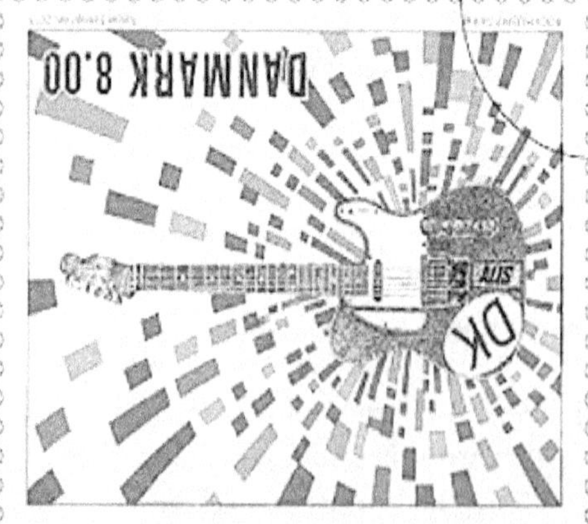

Gobshite Quarterly

Double Trouble / Issue 13 – Winter 2014

This issue is dedicated to the memory of:

Zvonko Bušić (23 Jan., 1946 — 1 Sept., 2013)

Lou Reed (2 Mar., 1942 — 27 Oct., 27, 2013)

Zvonko Bušić (23 Jan., 1946 — 1 Sept., 2013)

Lou Reed (2 Mar., 1942 — 27 Oct., 27, 2013)

This issue is dedicated to the memory of:

Double Trouble / Issue 14 – Spring 2014

Gobshite Quarterly

9.00 USDOL | | € 6.50 EURO | | £ 5.30 GBP (UK) | | $ 9.50 AUD (Oz) | | $9.00 CAN | | ¥ 870 JPY (japan yen) | | 85.00 SAR (S. Africa)

9.00 USDOL | | € 6.50 EURO | | £ 5.30 GBP (UK) | | $ 9.50 AUD (Oz) | | $9.00 CAN | | ¥ 870 JPY (japan yen) | | 85.00 SAR (S. Africa)

Gobshite Quarterly

Double Trouble / Issue 14 – Spring 2014

This issue is dedicated to the memory of:

Zvonko Bušić (23 Jan., 1946 — 1 Sept., 2013)

Lou Reed (2 Mar., 1942 — 27 Oct., 27, 2013)

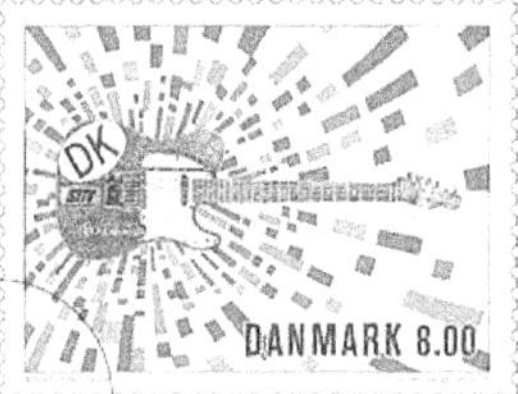

Portfolio / "Ice is nice...", photography, M. F. McAuliffe

The Usual Suspects
Staff

Editor R. V. Branham

Office Mgr. Sofia Sensei Satori Shostakovna Satyagraha Stolicniya Sashimi Shitkicker

Assoc. Editor M. F. McAuliffe

Contrib. Editors T. Warburton y Bajo & Channing Dodson & Arianna Morgan & Douglas Spangle

Design T. Warburton y Bajo

Cover Illo Graham K. Willoughby

Cover comix illos Sarah Laing & Wild eyed grp.

Photos M. F. McAuliffe, & T. Warburton y Bajo

Layout T. Warburton y Bajo & R. V. Branham

Design Assts. Channing Dodson & Arianna Morgan

Legal Peter Shaver

Publishers GobQ LLC/Reprobate Books

Post-production printing Ingram Spark/Lightning Source

P.R. P. H. Vazak

Gobshite Quaerterly: Double Trouble, Nos. 13/14, Winter & Spring 2014
ISBN 978-1-63068-139-5

Hitchcock font created by Matt Terich, based on the work of Saul Bass ... Avail. for download @ http://typographica.org/001110.php

GobQ volunteers: Qualified candidates please send résumé to our P.O. Box [GobQ. LLC, PO Box 11346, Portland, OR 97211] or to gobq@yahoo.com

Special thanks to Craig Florence, Michael Heald, Rhonda Hughes, Kevin Sampsell, & Curtis Whitecarrol

Copyright © 2013, by Gobshite Quarterly, GobQ LLC., Individual Contrib. Copyrights notwithstanding...

All rights reserved & tra la la & boo-fucking-hoo...

Respectfully flip the book over, as Issue 13, Winter 2014, is a whole upsy-daisy 48 pgs away fr. the centre

Gob Words A word to give offense, when offense may be due. ***Gobshite***, per OED, is what the American crew of Adm. Perry's Expedition to Japan were called by the natives; American Heritage Dictionary, 4th. ed., refers to a wad of expectorated chaw & to the Old Eng. *Shiten*; yet another dictionary refers to a Gobshite as a "*pernicious blatherskite*"—in other words, a stiff to read the teleprompter feed for CNN or for Rupert Murdoch's Fox "*News*" bullshit mountain. & these are the people offended by the word, so think before giving in to those who'd control speech (& by ext., thought). Indeed, why else are censors so vigorously censorious? Is this good or bad? Wasn't it Pulitzer who said that journalism should comfort the afflicted & afflict the comfortable? Quick, is this good or bad? (...& it hurts to have to ask, as this went to press in late fall, 2013, but... Has the federal government reopened) (Good or Bad?) One of our goals is to present the best writing fr. around the world, w/ works orig. published in another language presented *en face*. Quick, is this good or bad? & who decides? Quick...
— *rvb*

The Usual Suspects
Contributors

Kassten Alonso, born in Seatac, raised in Anchorage, & Eugene, lives in Portland w/ his wife & daughter; is a member of Spanbauer's Dangerous Writing workshop. *Core: a Romance*, published by Portland's Hawthorne Books, was a 2005 OR Book Awards finalist; his 2nd. novel, fresh fr. Fiction Collective 2, *The Pet Thief*, excerpted here.

Tomislav Marijan Bilosnić, Croatian writer, makes his *GobQ* debut w/ 4 pomes fr. his coll., *Wrought Silver*.

Tiffany Lee Brown, *Plazm* co-ed., & GobQ contrib., returns w/ *Another Poem*.

Wendy Chin-Tanner, whose poetry coll., *TURN*, is due in 2014, has work in journals incl. *The Raintown Rev.* & *the Mays Anthology of Oxford & Cambridge*; poetry ed. at *Stealing Time Mag.*, & *The Nervous Breakdown*. *Sunday* & *Full Moon* are her *GobQ* debuts.

Alexander Cigale is a NYC-based poet & translator; his own work & translations are in journals, incl. in *The Cafe*, *Colorado*, *Global City*, *Gargoyle*, *Hanging...*, & in *qarrtsiluni* & *Off Course*. He returns to *GobQ* w/ his *Ščerbina limericks* translations.

Jo Cook is a Vancover-based artist whose work has been invar. Canadian gallaeries; her visual narratives parkake of everything from comics to Pessoa; she returns to GobQ with *Town Without Pitty*.

Channing Dodson, a Portland-based kana-wrangler, returns to *GobQ* w/ another reasoned rant.

Friedrich Dürrenmatt (1921–1990) has been translated into several languages; his best-known works incl. the novel *The Pledge* (1958), made into a Sean Penn film in 2001. 2 pomes are in this issue.

Priscilla Galligan lives in Warren, RI, & works freelance as a researcher, & grant writer. *Murphy's Law* is her *GobQ* debut.

Dena Rash Guzman, based near Portland, OR, is founding ed. of *Unshod Quills*, & poetry ed. of HAL (Hong Kong-based indie publisher); her debut coll. is *Life Cycle*. Dena's *GobQ* debut is *The Greatest Famine in History* (orig. on *Ink Node*, 16 May, 2012).

Marilyn Hacker has written 9 books, incl.

the award-winning vols. *Winter Numbers*, *Desperanto*, & *Squares & Courtyards*, as well as a trans. of Vénus Khoury-Ghata's *She Says*. Hacker co-edited QUARK, a quarterly anthol., w/ Samuel R. Delany. She lives in NY & Paris. Her translations of Khoury-Ghata, Darwish, & Etienne have regularly been in GobQ; the Khoury-Ghata trans. here reprinted as a BestGob & excerpted fr. a pome-cycle in our debut.

Roman Karlović's translations of Tomislav Marijan Bilosnić's pomes are in *GobQ's* Winter & Spr. issues.

Vénus Khoury-Ghata, Lebanese poet & novelist, resides in Paris; author of a dozen vols. of poems & as many novels. She received the Prix Mallarmé & Prix Apollinaire for *Monologue du mort*, & for *Les Ombres et leurs cris*. Translated into Italian, Russian, Dutch, German, & Arabic, her collections incl. *She Says*, & *Compassion des pierres*. Her pomes & stories have been featured in several GobQ issues; the pome here reprinted as a BestGob & excerpted fr. a pome-cycle in our very first issue.

Sarah Laing lives in Auckland, NZ, w/ her 3 kids. She writes short stories, novels, & comics; her novel, *The Fall of Light*, is fr. Vintage NZ. Excerpted here is a w.i.p. about Katherine Mansfield & her.

Michael Lohr returns to *GobQ* w/ the urban anthro of *Ritual Offerings to the Taxi Gods*.

M. F. McAuliffe returns w/ 3 essays, fr. her *Knitting Alone For 1000s of Miles* blog.

Graham Murtaugh is a 3rd.-gen OR poet who also facilitates Write Around Portland workshops. His work's been in TriMet's Orange Lining Project, *Booth 5*, & *InkNode*. *Hunting at Low Tide* is his *GobQ* debut. Other work is avail. in this issue's E-zine ed.

Daniele Pantano is a Swiss writer & translator whose Dürrenmatt (*The Possible Is Monstrous: Selected Poems*) & Walser (*Oppressive Light: Selected Poems*) translations are incl. in *GobQ*.

Щербина / **Ščerbina** Limericks appear here *en face* w/ Alexander Cigale's translation.

Michael Shay , Portland based poet, returns w/ *For A Living*.

Douglas Spangle returns w/ a pome, *Her Camera*, fr. *A White Concrete Day, a new coll. fr. Reprobate/GobQ Books*.

Monica Storss, scribe & indie PR wallah, has worked w/ Literary Death Match, Sm. Press Distrib., & INK Books, & curates *Venom & the Anecdote* readings. Her pubs incl. *Unshod Quills & Rattlesnakes Rev. GobQ* is proud to welcome her.

Brenda Taulbee moved fr. Montana to Portland in 2012 & was invited to give her 1st. public poetry reading that Sept. in Stone Soup's Reading series. *When You Make Lemonade* is not only Brenda's *GobQ* debut, it is also her debut publication.

Robert Walser (1878—1956), born in Switzerland, left school at 14 & led a peripatetic, precarious existence while writing pomes, stories, essays, & 3 novels, incl: *The Tanners* (1906), & *The Assistant* (1908). In 1933 he abandoned writing & entered a sanatorium, where he resided the rest of his life. "*I am not here to write, but to be mad.*" *Oppressive Light: Selected Poems*, has bee receontly published. 2 pomes are incl. in this issue.

Graham Willoughby, whose artwork has adorned our covers since the 2nd. issue, again returns, w/ simpler, starker, but no less evocative covers for the Spr. 2014 issue, as well as for the Winter 2014 issue on the other side.

Town Without Pity

we look like dragoons here. rough.
first never trace how things happened
like he could be a butcher with no
words but lots uv scars. resign.
there are no weapons.

because she would
take him and ramp up or hardly at
all would be no brain sturgeons

please oh please don't tell the
sledgehammer. i don't want to go back.
ok i do. past thee hem & haw. how's she ever going to own a private roam?

i know there are
other people but
i don't know where
they are if i could
find them about
being scared - if
they are. blame me.
tonight early out
beans for cover

little kids playing
around the pits
until dark none of
them being particularly
competitive.   when it's
time Nut & Barker
come out
to lead the
way home

rutalg is
calling me
i can
hear him
from the
listening
hole

no doubt
what's lacking
is party hats

leg over. rump under. steak & kidney pie
flip yr wig. blow yr cool. poke 'em in the eye

blowing
the worm
is the
name
uv
the
game
OK?

i know about the day
uv busted heads. i
know we're being
spied on by the veilers
& i know you know where
to find donuts.

rat boy wrote a
spectacle for 3 voices
never wanted

or anyone else until
i didn't believe regularly

people goes
under wonder
butt. how
at first
she were
looping
slightly
dependent or
whatever was
mutual

just bits
baby she
sed pull
it out

on day 30 we'll
be given clean
clothes & we'll
turn our backs
on doorkeeper
stinker

Jo Cook

Little Beirut, Oregon

Hunting at Low Tide

To what extent is it like swallowing a live octopus? Tentacles, teeth, slick orange unraveling. Briny slide. It tangles into a vascular kind of fight; coral roots in the reef of the chest. The lungs: suspicious angelfish. What remains at the heart's low tide? Black ink and blood. A tiny beak on a string, worn around the neck. Two mouths. Four hearts. Victorious.

— *Graham Murtaugh*

Zagreb, Hrvatska / Croatia

Dijete, ubrizgaj mi morfij

Prestao sam putovati, bilo je jutro i toplo,
kopracao sam se s metkom u prsima.

Poslije sto tisuća godina
kemijom se vratio
u raspršivaču.
Hoću li neozlijeđen
između dviju zvijezda proći,
ili ću ubiti njihove krijesnice?

Uključili su tv i infuziju,
jezik je postao metalan.
Dijete, ubrizgaj mi morfij da opet spavam,
ne osjećam predmete,
ne razumijem ih ni najmanje.

– *Tomislav Marijan Bilosnić*

Little Beirut, Oregon

KID, GIVE ME A MORPHINE INJECTION

My journey was over, it was morning and warm.
I wriggled with a bullet in my chest.

Came back chemically
in a spray
a hundred thousand years on.
Will I manage to squeeze through
the two stars unhurt,
or do I kill their glowworms?

They've turned on the TV and the infusion pump,
and my tongue tastes like metal.
Kid, give me a morphine injection
so I can sleep some more.
I'm numb to the things around me,
don't understand them at all.

— *Trans., Roman Karlović*

Portfolio / Japanese Gate, Max Expo Centre Sta., photography, M. F. McAuliffe

Every Edge A Centre:Another Day in Hebron, Palestinian Authory-Controlled West Bank

It was nearly eight o'clock on a Thursday morning in early January, and my wife and I were speeding haphazardly through the streets of Jerusalem in a taxi. We couldn't afford to be late, and I had thought about asking the driver to step on it, but a few moments careening through the morning traffic indicated to me that this was not really necessary or advisable. We pulled up in front of the King David Hotel with not a moment to spare and rushed across the street to the parking lot of the YMCA where we saw a few young women standing near an old, white Toyota minivan. One of them, short with shoulder-length blonde hair and looking uncomfortably cold in spite of wearing a heavy black leather jacket, walked over to us clutching a clipboard close to her chest. "Hi," she said in Hebrew-accented English, "Are you here for the tour?"

The tour in question was a tour of Hebron in the Palestinian Authority-controlled sections of the West Bank and was run by an Israeli company called Green Olive Tours. My wife had been to Israel half a dozen times before for work or to visit family and friends but had never consciously traveled in the West Bank. (Later, she realized that a few of the places she had visited on previous trips had, in fact, been over the Green Line or involved traveling across it to or from other places.) This was my first visit to Israel, and having been sucked down the wormhole of Israel-Palestine-related media, I wanted our two-week trip to Israel to include a visit to Palestine as well. My wife, genuinely curious but also a bit uneasy, agreed.

I honestly didn't know what to expect. The night before the tour, I sat up late with our Air BnB host in Jerusalem, who had mentioned that he spent two years of his army service stationed in the West Bank. He was excited that we would be stopping in Bethlehem, which he told us was an increasingly modern and cosmopolitan Arab city. "You'll have fun," he said with a smile before I went off to bed.

The Israeli woman by the van handed us a couple of booklets before leaving and turning us over to the driver, a young Arab Israeli man. Along with my wife and I, the others on the tour were Heike, a young German woman who lived in Copenhagen with her Israeli boyfriend, and Jeanne, a young French woman who lived in London. Heike had been to Israel a few times before, but it was Jeanne's first trip. The two of them had been on a tour of Ramallah with Green Olive the other day and liked it so much that they decided to do this tour as well. Apparently, one more person would be joining our group after we crossed into the West Bank.

As the van headed south, I read through the short potted history of the Arab-Israeli conflict contained in the booklet. Written by "the Green Olive Team," I thought it did a relatively good job of explaining the historic stages of the conflict from the first arrival of Jew-

ish settlers from Europe to the Ottoman sanjaks in the 1880s, to the formation of the present shape and boundaries of Israel/Palestine when Britain split its mandate territory into Palestine and Transjordan in 1921, to the more recent stages of civil war, inter-ethnic conflict, occupation, and terror attacks. Though it exuded some pro-Palestinian sympathies, nothing really raised my eyebrows until I came to a line near the end where it said that Yasser Arafat "died while under Israeli siege in his Ramallah office" near the end of the Second Intifada. (In reality, he died in a Paris hospital in 2004.) Upon reading this, my wife gave me a nervous look.

After about 20 minutes on the road, we pulled up to a checkpoint. We had been told to bring our passports, but the Border Police officer at the checkpoint quickly glanced through the window at us, exchanged a few words with the driver, and waved us through.

Winding upward through the Judean hills, it didn't take long before we spotted Israeli settlements on the hilltops across from us. There were also large red signs with white letters in Hebrew, Arabic and English that stated that the road we were traveling on was in Palestinian-controlled Area A. For Israeli citizens, driving here was "a danger to your life and illegal under Israeli law." Shortly afterwards, we parked in a Palestinian city, got out, and were led to a small tourist information office. The driver then got back in the van and drove away. After waiting for a few minutes and wondering what exactly was going on, we were met by George, our tall, balding, chain-smoking Palestinian guide, along with the final member of our group, Graham, a Canadian in his mid-20s who lived in Switzerland and had been staying at George's home and traveling around the West Bank for the past few days. George explained to us that he worked for the Alternative Tourism Group (ATG), a Palestinian company that was sponsored by the Lutheran Church and worked in cooperation with Green Olive to bring tourists to Palestine. After giving us a 10-minute overview of what we would see that day, we got in another white Toyota minivan and headed south.

As we drove, George told us that the city we had just been in was his hometown of Beit Sahour (pop. 14,000), the only city with a Christian majority in Palestine. Its name meant "house of the shepherd," and it was supposedly from here that the shepherds guarding their flocks were guided to the manger in Bethlehem. Just outside of Bethlehem, a large Israeli settlement with its distinct, neat, semi-circular rows of white buildings with reddish-brown rooftops came into view. This was the Israeli settlement of Efrat, George explained. A little ways away to our left, we passed a newly-planted Palestinian olive grove and next to it, a much smaller Israeli settlement of about two dozen portable homes. I asked George whether these homes were legal under Israeli law or whether they were one of the growing number of illegal outposts that had sprung up in recent years. After pointing out the interesting nature of my question (from a Palestinian perspective, all of the settlements are illegal under international law), he shrugged and said that he thought they were "legal."

While taking the van around increas-

ingly precarious turns at high speed, George focused on promoting Palestine's case for international recognition and independence, and his personal feelings quickly came to the surface. Coming from a Christian family (though outspokenly anti-religion by this point in his life), he hated Hamas and their brand of Islamic extremism. To our surprise, he did not even want Gaza to be a part of the new Palestinian state. "What I would like to see is a secular, democratic Palestinian state in the West Bank and East Jerusalem," he said. "Egypt can take Gaza." When I pointed out that Gazans probably wouldn't like that idea, he said they could just sort out their own problems under Hamas rule. "Before 2006, I used to go to Gaza almost every week. Many West Bank families went there on vacations to go to the beach. Today, I would never go to Gaza, and I would never allow anyone in my family to go to Gaza," he said somewhat bitterly. In his view, the extremists on both sides of the conflict fed off of one another: "Every violent act from Hamas and even more extreme groups like the Salafists only makes the Occupation stronger. It gives the Israelis an excuse to hurt all of us. This is not real resistance!" he shouted, waving his right hand in the air while steering the van around jagged switchback turns with his left. "Real resistance is education."

↖ ↗ ↙ ↘

After the obligatory stop at the Church of the Nativity in Bethlehem, we got back in the van and he drove us to the West Bank barrier (a.k.a. the "security fence," a.k.a. "the apartheid wall"). Driving from Nazareth to Jerusalem a few days earlier, I had seen some sections of it from the highway, and it looked like just an innocuous fence with some barbed wire running along the top. Near Bethlehem, the appearance was decidedly more severe as thick concrete walls and guard towers cut their way through the disorganized urban landscape. Despite its imposing appearance, it still looked smaller than what I had expected from photographs. Graffiti in dozens of languages covered the wall. As I walked up the street, I turned a corner and saw "Freedom for Palestine" written in Japanese. A few paces further and we came to a small storefront across from the wall called "Banksy's Shop." Named for the Bristol graffiti artist who helped make the wall famous with his tags, locals were now profiting off his work by selling t-shirt reproductions, photos, and postcards. I only saw one actual Banksy stencil on the wall itself—a picture of a girl floating away holding a bunch of balloons—but Graham suspected that it wasn't original. Sensing that we weren't quite satisfied, George droves us down the road to the Behtlehem Intercontinental Hotel, across from which was one of Banksy's most famous tags, a picture of a little girl with pigtails in a yellow dress frisking an Israeli soldier. Up the street from the hotel, three Palestinian Authority security guards in green uniforms with rifles slung over their shoulders milled around on the street corner smoking cigarettes and looking like they had nothing in the world to do.

A short distance away, we stopped at the Aida Refugee Camp. While "refugee camp" would normally conjure up tents, field hospitals, and soup kitchens, U.N.-sponsored camps like this one are indistinguishable from other neighborhoods. The primary difference is that

residents carry special ID cards denoting that they are refugees or the descendents of refugees who fled in 1948. They will carry these cards until a settlement is reached with the Israeli government over lost property claims. Aida was incredibly dirty, its streets strewn with garbage and the pockmarks of bullets visible on many buildings. A mural on the barrier wall directly opposite the camp showed teenage boys with slings throwing stones at Israeli soldiers while other soldiers took a blindfolded boy away. One soldier's face had been painted over with a disturbing splash of red paint. The three nearby guard towers visible along the wall were all heavily blackened from repeated firebombing. In an alleyway, seven young Palestinian boys, all under the age of ten, chased each other and played with marbles underneath a large mural of the iconic PFLP airline hijacker Leila Khaled, clad in a hijab and clutching an AK-47. A caption above it in English read "Leila Khaled For Ever." When I pulled out my phone to take a picture of the boys, they instantly assembled in two rows, smiled, and waved their arms in the air. Only after I left did it occur to me that maybe they were hoping I'd give them some money.

It was now midday, and George drove us a further 20 or so minutes south to Hebron. On the way, I noticed several signs by the side of the road for Otzma l'Israel ("Power to Israel"), a xenophobic pro-settlement party running in the upcoming Israeli elections later that month. (Fortunately, they failed to win any seats.)

Our first stop in Hebron was the Natsheh family's glass-blowing studio. We watched with awe as a young man deftly blew and worked molten glass into a vase. In another room, other workers painted elaborate designs on tiles and plates. Huge stacks of plates and trivets had "*Shalom*" written on then in Hebrew and Roman letters. They can be found in virtually every souvenir shop in Israel, but we hadn't realized that they were made here. My wife and I wanted to buy something, but we had no idea how we'd ever get it home.

Piling back in the van, George drove us to the old city of Hebron, arguably one of the most contentious epicenters of the Israeli-Palestinian conflict. With more than 230,000 residents, Hebron is the only place in the West Bank where Israeli settlers actually live in an Arab city. The city is divided into the larger Palestinian-controlled H1 sector, and the smaller Israeli-controlled H2 sector around the old city, where some 700 Israeli settlers live among 30,000 Palestinians.

Walking through the old souk, netting was strung up overhead to protect people from garbage thrown by settlers who lived in the apartments above. A faded and frayed Israeli flag could be seen flying from a window above us. I stopped by a fruit vendor and bought a mix of pomegranate and orange juice. At two shekels for a large glass, it was much cheaper than in the Old City in Jerusalem. It tasted fresher, too. For all of its heavy atmosphere, I was beginning to like Hebron; it seemed a bit like a miniaturized version of the Old City but with far fewer tourists.

Two young boys followed us through the souk shoving rubber wristbands with Palestinian flags on them in our faces. Despite repeatedly telling them "La, shukran" ("No, thank you") and waving them away, they persistently continued to follow us. Shopkeepers eyed us excit-

edly and shouted, "Welcome! Welcome! Whereyoufrom?" I made the mistake of stopping to eye some of the antiques in one shop. The owner quickly rushed up to me and showed me an old British Mandate-era coin with "Palestine" written on it in Arabic, Hebrew, and English. I asked how much he wanted for it. "200 shekels," he said. I declined, thanked him, and tried to catch up with the group, but he ran after me and grabbed me hard by my arm, trying to talk me into a deal. He followed me a good fifty yards and was offering the coin for 50 shekels before he finally gave up. Unlike in the Old City of Jerusalem or Bethlehem, shopkeepers here have no steady supply of tourists to count on.

We exited the souk through a checkpoint manned by a few Israeli Border Police, all but one of them Ethiopian Israelis. From the looks on their faces, I got the sense that they'd rather be anywhere in the world but here. The souk exit opened out onto a wide stone path up the hill to Al Haram Al Ibrahimi, the Muslim mosque built at the time of Saladin over a Herodian mausoleum covering the Cave of the Patriarchs, the site where Abraham, Sarah, Isaac, Jacob, Leah, and Rebecca were all reputedly buried. Today, the mosque is divided into a Muslim side and a Jewish side, which has been converted into a synagogue. Jews are only permitted to enter the Muslim side on 12 days of the year and vice-versa. My wife and I were a little concerned about this because a rabbi we knew was barred from entering the mosque earlier that year when a Border Police officer noticed her star of David necklace. I happened to have a kippa in my pocket for when we entered the synagogue side. George assured us that there was no problem. "As far as I know, you are all American and European Christian tourists, and that is what I will tell the guards," he said with a wink. As we were waived through a second checkpoint at the mosque entrance, I saw an Israeli Border Police officer chatting with some Palestinian children. He said something to them in Arabic and handed them some candy from his pocket. The children took the candy, giggled, and ran away.

My wife had brought a scarf to use as a hijab, but in addition to this, the women were required to don large "modesty cloaks," the pointed tops of which made them look a bit like coneheaded extras from a science fiction movie.

As it was between prayers, the mosque was mostly empty. We stopped in front of a large stone cenotaph covered with green cloth. This was where Isaac was buried, George said. On the other side of the hall was an intricately ornamented wooden pulpit inlaid with gold. Apparently, it dated from the time of Saladin—one of few such artifacts to survive from that time. As we walked, George told us about the massacre that occurred where we were standing on Purim in 1994. Baruch Goldstein, an American-Israeli follower of Meir Kahane who served as a medic in the IDF, walked into the mosque with an assault rifle and grenades, killing 29 people and wounding dozens more before he was overpowered and beaten to death. George was convinced that given the level of carnage, Goldstein had not acted alone and Israel was covering up the full story. I stared at the emerald green walls, red prayer rugs, and ornate geometric patterns and Quranic calligraphy covering

the walls and ceiling, in the serene site of an atrocity. A metal grate on a window dividing the mosque from the synagogue on the other side was the only visible sign of the tension that lingered beneath the surface.

On our way out, we met a teenager named Ahmed, a native of the city and a friend of George's. As part of the tour, Ahmed's family had agreed to host us for lunch in their home. We walked down the hill and across the street to the shop owned by Ahmed's father and the family's home above it. As I walked, I noticed a line of Israeli police barricades lining the path and on the other side of them a medium-sized two-storey bulding called the Sde HaMachpela, the visitor's center for the Jewish synagogue side. All of the cars in the parking lot had Israeli plates, and two Border Police stood by the barricades.

The family treated us to a delicious lunch of grilled chicken, rice pilaf, salad, and yogurt. Ahmed's mother proudly showed us a picture of her oldest daughter graduating from Al Quds University. A stern photograph of Ahmed's late grandmother hung over the mantle. Everyone feared and respected her in Hebron, George told us—even the Israeli army.

As we came back out onto the street, George and Ahmed said that they would meet up with us after we came out of the synagogue. George was sauntering away and lighting what seemed like his fiftieth cigarette of the day when suddenly, we heard a child screaming, and George and Ahmed rushed across the street to see what was happening. A mother was crying hysterically as her three-year-old daughter screamed in pain, blood gushing from her finger. Apparently, she had been playing with some other children and had sliced the tip of one of her fingers off somehow. The two Border Police rushed over and one of them joined a group of local men scouring the ground looking for the errant bit of flesh. The other radioed his commanding officer, asking permission for the family to bring a car around to pick the girl up. "It's a little girl!" I heard him shout in Hebrew. I couldn't hear the reply, but the man's ashen face said it all. The request had been denied. The Border Police officer apologetically explained the situation to Ahmed and the girl's father, who quickly picked her up and ran up the hill around the back of the mosque and the souk to Ahmed's car to take the girl to the hospital. It was only after they left that I noticed that there was a Magen David Adom ambulance sitting in the Sde HaMachpela parking lot a mere 100 feet away. Later, when we told Israeli friends and family about our time in Hebron, this was the part of the story that most deeply upset them. "Why didn't anyone think to find the ambulance personnel?" they would ask. Settlement or not, they were required to help anyone in need of medical attention. As we walked back up the hill, a bloodstained paper towel blew past us in the breeze.

Standing on the other side of the police barricade, there was a sign in Hebrew that read "Welcome to Hebron: City of the Patriarchs!" Near the top of the steps leading to the synagogue entrance was a sign denoting the famous "seventh step" that read:

The Seventh Step

Following the Mamluk conquest of Eretz Yisrael in 1267, the conquering Islamic regime forbade Jews to enter the edifice over the Tomb of the Patriarchs. Jewish access was confined to the seventh

step leading up to the eastern entrance. There Jews prayed for seven hundred years. On June 8, 1967, Hebron was liberated, and the Jews returned to their Patriarchal possession. The gate and steps by which Jews had been humiliated for hundreds of years were removed by the Head of the Central Command, General Revahem Zeevi in 1969. All the same, many Jews still pray at that site, which has been hallowed by the prayers and tears of countless generations.

↖ ↗ ↙ ↘

This was certainly contentious ground, to say the least.

A Jewish man stood praying nearby. Were it not for his knit kippa and flaming red peyos, I would have taken him for a hippie rather than a Jewish settler. Inside, the synagogue was visually the same as the adjoining mosque on the other side. Aside from some velvet wall hangings covering Quranic inscriptions, the Jewish occupants had made no attempt to alter the space. The only English written anywhere was the names of rich American Jews who had made donations. The metal grates in front of some of the cenotaphs were the mirror image of those on the mosque side, but at least here, I could read the inscriptions hanging from them: Avraham avinu (Abraham our father), Ya'akov avinu (Jacob our father), Leah imenu (Leah our mother.) A Jewish man stood praying before a wall covered in ornate Arabic calligraphy. Turning a corner, I saw two Ethiopian Jewish teenagers studying Talmud with a gray-bearded Ashkenazi teacher. Near the exit, we came to a cenotaph that had no inscription. My wife and I asked a nearby Haredi man in our faltering Hebrew who was buried there. He said that he wasn't sure, but that he thought it was Esav (Esau). "Where are you from?" he asked in Hebrew. I replied that we were visiting from America. "I can give you a tour for a little money," he said. "Money?" I asked. "For the children," he replied. I politely declined.

It was only when we came back down the hill that I understood why the incident with the little girl had been so problematic. The street at the bottom of the hill was Shuhada Street, which was closed off to Palestinians. After a group of settlers had been attacked there in 2000, local shopkeepers and residents refused to cooperate with IDF investigators. In response, dozens of shops were closed and hundreds of people forcibly evicted. The street was now like something out of a ghost town. About halfway down the street was a large hand-painted banner for the Otzma l'Yisrael party that read "No duties, no rights!" an apparent reference to Arab Israelis' exemption from national service in Israel. Nearby was a sign in Hebrew and English that read "These stores were closed by the IDF for Security reasons after the Arabs began the *Oslo War* (aka the Second Intifada) in September of 2000, attacking, wounding, and murdering Jews on this road." A few doors further down was a memorial plaque with a faded photograph of a young Orthodox couple, apparently two of the victims killed in the attack. The memorial was directly across the street from a Muslim cemetery. As I turned around to head back, I saw a group of settler children walking home from school at the far end of the street.

By now it was after four, and the sun was fading. George began driving us

back, but before we left Hebron, he took us to see a keffiyeh factory on the outskirts of the city. Apparently, it was the only one still operating in Palestine. Most of the keffiyehs sold today were made in China, he said. George stayed outside and pulled a new packet of Gauloises from his jacket pocket. Inside, the factory was deserted, but electric looms spun, whirred, and clacked away while a large portrait of Yasser Arafat flanked by Palestinian and French flags beamed down approvingly.

We drove back to Beit Sahour, and George invited us into his home to wait for the other van to take us back to Israel. His high school-aged daughter brought us water and soda. From the balcony, there was an extraordinary view across the valley floor to the Judean hills beyond punctuated by the settlement of Har Homa straight across from us, looming like a whitewashed castle over the hillside.

The van came and took us back, and we walked with Heike and Jeanne back to the city center. Given what we'd seen, they seemed surprisingly upbeat and cheerful and talked of maybe going on another tour. We parted ways and walked back to the apartment where we were staying just off of the Jaffa Road. My wife was exhausted, but I felt like I needed to clear my head and went out for a walk. It was a Thursday night, and the pedestrian thoroughfares of the Jaffa Road and Ben Yehuda Street were bursting with people out for a night of pre-Shabbat revelry. Laughter, conversation, and the sound of buskers with out-of-tune guitars filled the air. I stood in the center of the street and realized that all this was less than 20 miles from Hebron, but it felt like it may as well have been on another planet.

— *Channing Dodson*

↖ ↗ ↙ ↘

WHEN YOU MAKE LEMONADE:

in last night's shot glass
mix equal parts regret and
don't-give-a-fuck.
pluck the fruit that looks most
like the sun,

pretend the universe
could unbecome in your hands.

carefully remove every seed.
there's no need to grow
any more bitter. frost your tongue
with sugar, chew a hole
through the rind like every
safety net you've designed
your escape from.

squeeze. repeat.

— *Brenda Taulbee*

SCHWEIZERPSALM III

Einst dürstete ich nach deinem Glauben
  Mein Land
Nun dürste ich nach deiner Gerechtigkeit
  Wahrlich
Die Ärsche deiner Staatsanwälte und Richter
  Lasten so schwer auf ihr
Daß ich das Wort Freiheit kaum mehr ertragen kann
  Das du ständig im Maule führst
Deine Glaubhaftigkeit zu beweisen
  An die niemand mehr glaubt
Nur noch deine Bankgeheimnisse sind glaubhaft.
Was ist aus dir geworden, mein Land?

Wenn du morgens für die Neger in Biafra und
  anderswo Geld sammelst
Legst du dich, Bet- und Bettschester zugleich,
  Abends mit deren Häuptlingen zwischen die Laken
Deine Waffengeschäfte abschließend
  Damit jene, mit denen du schläfst,
Die abknallen, für die du gesammelt hast,
  Und wenn man deine Zuhälter faßt
Wissen sie von nichts.

Von den Steuerhinterziehern aller Länder unterhalten
  Schenkst du general Westmoreland Whisky ein
Mit ihm nächtlich auf die Rettung des Abendlandes
  anstoßend.

Wehe denen, die anders denken als du
  Deine Lehrstühle
Hältst du von jedem Stäubchen Marxismus rein
  Dein Patriotismus ist so steril und keimfrei
Daß auf seinem Boden wirklich nichts mehr wächst
  Jede neue Idee ist für dich eine Seuche
So lebst du in ewiger Furcht vor Schnupfen und Masern
  Dabei hast du Krebs, du willst es nur nicht wissen,

SWISS PSALM III

I once thirsted after your faith
My country
Now I thirst after your justice
Truly
The asses of your attorneys and judges
Weigh so heavily on her
That I can hardly bear the word "Freedom"
You constantly carry in your mouth
To prove your trustworthiness
In which nobody believes anymore
Only the bank secrets are still credible.
What happened to you, my country?

In the mornings when you collect money
for the negroes in Biafra and elsewhere
You lie, as a sister in prayer and bed,
With their chiefs between the sheets at night,
Sealing your weapon deals
So that those with whom you sleep
Kill those for whom you raised funds,
And when your pimps are caught,
They don't know about anything.

Supported by tax evaders
Of all countries, you pour
General Westmoreland whiskey
And toast to the rescue of the West.

Woe to those who think differently
You keep your universities clean
From every mote of Marxism
Your patriotism is so sterile and aseptic
That absolutely nothing grows in its soil
Every new idea is a plague
Thus you live in constant fear
Of the cold and measles

Und die Psychiater kratzen sich velegen hinter den Ohren
   Reden sie von dir, doch du läßt nicht mit dir reden
Wer dir seine Moral predigen will
   Den läßt du deine Moral spüren.

Nichts gegen deine Armee. Dieser wackere Verein
   Verdrosch einst Österreicher, Burgunder und Deutsche
Verdrosch die Unterdrückten fremder Unterdrücker
   Doch vor allem verdrosch er sich selber
Bis er von Napoleon gottseidank so gründlich verdroschen wurde
   Daß er seitdem friedlicher wurde
Unsere Grenzen mit seinen Waffen beschützend
   Wie er sich einbildet
Denn in Wahrheit wurden wir hauptsächlich
   Durch unsere Geschäfte beschützt.

Nichts gegen diesen Verein. Man tritt
   Ihm unfreiwillig bei, steht in den Statuten
Doch, wenn er sich an jenen vergreift
   Die diese nicht mehr unbedingt notwendig finden
Greife ich ihn an
   Im Namen der Freiheit
Die er zu verteidigen vorgibt.
Er ist nicht die Stütze meines Landes.
Die Stütze meines Landes sind die, welche denken
   Nicht jene, die mitmarschieren.

Armer Villard
   Das Töten verurteilend
Wirst du von einem Lande verurteilt
   Das aus dem Töten Profit zieht.
Deine Lauterkeit sei unser Vorbild.
Deine Tapferkeit werde die unsrige.
Die Tapferkeit, in einem Lande zu leben
   In welchem es langsam genierlich wird
Einem Bundesrat die Hand zu reichen.
Noch sind Wenige, die denken, doch die Mehrheit

Yet in fact you have cancer but don't
   Want to hear about it
And the psychiatrists, embarrassed, scratch their heads
   And talk about you, but you don't listen
To whomever is preaching his morality,
   you'll make your morality felt.

Nothing against your army. This brave club
Once thrashed Austrians, Burgunds and Germans
Thrashed the oppressed of foreign oppressors
   But they thrashed themselves, especially,
Until, thank God, Napoleon gave them such a thorough
   Thrashing, they since turned peaceful
Protecting our borders with its weapons
   How conceited
When in truth we were protected
   By our business affairs.

Nothing against this club. One joins
   Involuntarily, state the bylaws,
But when it assaults those
   Who find them no longer necessary,
I attack it
   In the name of freedom
It pretends to defend.
It doesn't support my country.
The support of my country are those who think
   Not those who march along.

Poor Villard
   Condemning murder, you are
Condemned by a country
   That profits from murder.
Your integrity shall be our example.
Your courage will be ours.
The courage to live in a country
   Where it becomes embarrassing
To shake a federal councilor's hand.

Stampft sie in den Untergrund
Stempelt sie zu Kanalisationsschweizern. So
Untergraben sie denn als Maulwürfe
Den Boden, der dich trägt, mein Land
Verändernd mit der Zeit
Was du unveränderlich hältst
Einen besudelten Schweizerpaß in der Tasche.

— Friedrich Dürrenmatt

Elektronische Hirne

Noch sind sie unsere Knechte
Noch führen sie aus
Was wir ihnen vorschreiben
Dumm, stur, emsig

Aber schon sind die Resultate
Die sie liefern
Nicht mehr zu kontrollieren
Nur durch ihresgleichen

Doch bald
Werden sie weiter rechnen
Ohne uns
Formeln finden,
die nicht mehr zu interpretieren sind

Bis sie endlich Gott erkennen,
ohne ihn zu verstehen
Schuld- und erbarmungslos
Straf- und rostfrei
Gefallene Engel

— Friedrich Dürrenmatt

There're only a few who think, but the majority
Stomps them into the underground
And labels them "Sewage-Swiss." So
As moles they undermine the ground
That carries you, my country,
Over time changing
What you believe unchangeable,
A soiled Swiss passport in their pockets.

— Trans., Daniele Pantano

NOTE: *Arthur Villard (1917-1995) was a teacher, socialist, & member of the National Council fr. 1971 to 1979. Although not an opponent of the Swiss army, he protested against its prosecution of conscientious objectors & as a result was himself jailed at the beginning of the 1960s.*

ELECTRIC BRAINS

They're still our servants
They still perform
What we command
Dumb, stubborn, diligent

But already the results
They deliver
Are uncontrollable
Except for the likes of them

And soon
They'll continue to calculate
Without us
Find formulas
That are no longer interpretable

Until they finally detect God
Without understanding Him
Innocent and merciless
Unpunished and rust free
Fallen angels

— Trans., Daniele Pantano

Ritual Offerings To The Taxi Gods

Michael Lohr

According to sources an estimated 27,000 laptop computers, 61,450 handheld computers and 402,000 mobile telephones were left in taxis around the world during the past year. But what is even more odd is that 616 artificial limbs were also left in cabs, as were 39 family pets, mostly cats and small dogs, but there were also two cases of pot-bellied pigs, a boa constrictor and a canary left behind. Worse yet, there were 14 instances of children being left to fend for themselves.

Taxi drivers in nine US cities also reported finding an unbelievable range of other items left behind by hurried passengers. The diverse collection of seemingly disposable relics of modern living included a concert harp, 41 unopened bottles of vermouth, 91 pairs of dentures, 1,017 sex toys, 142 pairs of shoes and 211 firearms. One taxi driver in Austin, Texas found a loaded 16 gauge shotgun with a laser scope just sitting in the backseat. One driver from Los Angeles reported finding a caged Bengal tiger cub in his taxi. The most valuable item discovered was a Roman Republic gold denarius minted during Emperor Vespasian's reign in 73AD. A patron left the coin in the back seat after attending an auction at Christie's Auction House in London.

The cab company reports document that a majority of the lost items were returned to their rightful owners. Eight out of ten mobile phones and 19 out of every 20 laptop computers were returned.

The statistics indicate that Londoners are more careless than others with their laptops. While Danes are most likely to forget their mobile phones, and believe it or not, the US is where you will most likely encounter a gun, used needle syringe, switchblade or other such dangerous implements lying in a cab. There were over 14,000 knives discovered in New York City cabs alone last year. Las Vegas and Los Angeles tied for first on the place were you will most likely have a grimy cab encounter with a sex toy, sexually explicit magazine or other related paraphernalia.

More bizarrely, there have also been 121 purported cases worldwide of taxis that were said to be haunted, most of these cases were in London and Cardiff. However, there is one case in Edinburgh, Scotland of an actual human skull being found. Police think it came from the university cadaver reserves or biology/physiology lab. Q

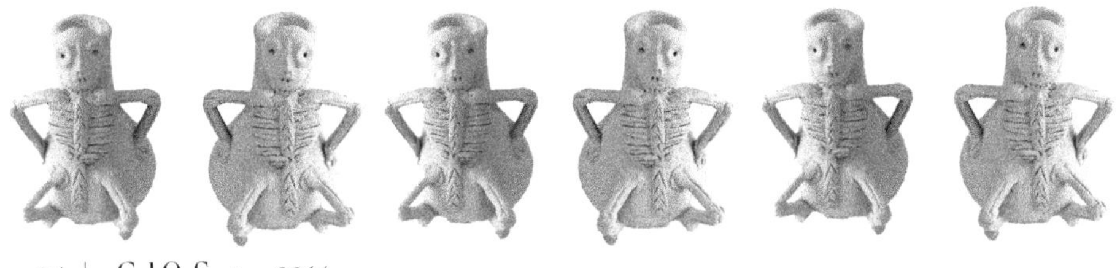

The Pet Thief (One)

Kassten Alonso

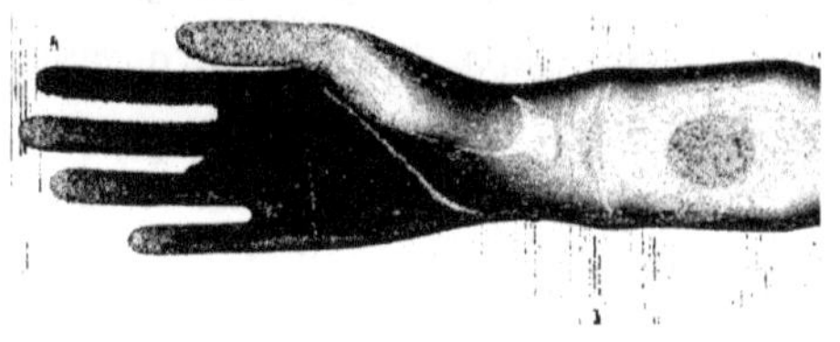

Tsokka tsokka tsokka.

Running comes. Tsokka tsokka tsokka tsokka. Black boots run. Huh huh red lips puff Huh huh Little fists swing Torn red stockings tic toc tic toc tic tocking. Long brown coat flaflaflap. Allee puddles Black boots splash. Pale throat, black collar Yellow tail wags Red mouth hollers Tsokka tsokka tsokka tsokka tsokka tsokka tsokka.

Allee splits. Corner bricks. Black boots cht cht cht Hand slaps bricks Brown coat spins Red stockings kick Gravel allee Black boots slip, run run run. Yellow tail fish flash sunlight.

Bee bee bee cars redgreenwhite.

Little brown coat black boots byebye.

Komp Komp Komp. Black shoes come. Komp komp komp. Black cap blue shirt Komp komp komp komp. Allee splits. Stone allee. Gravel allee. Clotheslines. Green shutters.

Cheeks blow huh, huh, huh. Merde.

Blue shirt bows. Black trouser knees sparkly hands grab. Ouaa.

Ouaaaaa. Sparkly cheeks nose pour onions salami brie.

Alors. Blue shirt tummy puffs big, little, big, little. Spits sour. Black cap turns. Black shoes come. My finger Doberman puppy tooths gnaw. Kick kick, little brown paws. Gravel allee.

Spinny top Blue shirt hides, babump babump babump. Scratches, big black shoes. Dirty black trouser turnups.

Alors. black shoes says. Which way she go. A droit. A gauche. The blonde. Hep. Im talkin to you. My tootsies Dusty shoe touches. Hollers come my head my fist hits. Foot kicks.

Cest quoi ce connn Door swings, flashes, Jinglelee Brown shoes come Green sweater Wrinkly hands Bon jour, officer. Mister says. May I help you.

I ask your grandson he saw my suspect, but he does not respond. huffing black cap says. Babump babump babump. Chin drips. Brown eyes my eyes. Hurt. Brown eyes get big.

Why does he yell. Im the one got kicked.

Grey trousers crouch. Grappa. Tobacco. Pink tummy spotted wrinkly hand pats. Yellow fingernails. Shiver. Shshsh. Its okay, my boy. Okay. Okay. My, this little puppy sure is happy, isnt he. What fun, to chew soft pink fingers, yes. Its okay, my boy.

Come on, kid, shes gettin away. says huffing blue shirt.

Mister says, Im afraid he couldnt tell you anything if he wanted to. He cant speak.

Well you can damn well point cant you.

Officer. Take a moment. Le regarder. Comprenez.

Hm. You got one of those, then. says trouser hips hands. Maybe you seen the girl, eh, Granpapa. Blonde, brown leather coat.

No, Officer, Im sorKomp komp komp komp komp komp. Running blue shirt black trousers black shoes get little. Little black cap turns sidetoside. Red neck hand rubs. Shoulders shrug. Merde alors. Little black cap Hand throws. Little redwhite-green cars zoum zoum.

Little blue shirt arm shakes, hollers, What good are you.

Mister rises. Lets go inside now. O dear. The puppys into something over there. Here, dont eat that. Eeesh.

Peanut butter biscuit my fingers show. Doberman pup whines. No. My lap panting pup lies. Furry head my hand cradles. Pink tummy cries. Pink tummy my hand rubs slow, Sososo. Brown eye, my eye. Moonpie, brown eye shows. Blink blink. Dry nose.

Cui cui cui. Cage birds hop.

Jinglee. says bell. Rain. Wind blows.

Wood stool creaks. Ahem. Bon soir, miss. Horrible wet out tonight, yes. The door, allow me.

Jingleelee. says bell. Shop door shuts. Pink hurty tummy my hand rubs. Little hidey top spins t ta, t ta, t ta, t ta. My fingers little tongue licks. Tongue pink, rough. Thirsty.

Clic. Clac. Clic. Clac. Clic. Fish tanks, cages, black boots stalk. Cheep cheep. Clic clac clic. Clic clac clic. Clic clac boots come.

Ach, O boy. says Pretty Boyd. Cat drags self in. Ha ha.

Pink tummy whines. Green bird bottle my hand takes. Metal spout shines. Soft black muzzle metal spout rubs.

Clic clac clic. Wet black boots. Long brown coat. Red stockings, wet. Black collar, white throat. Metal tag clinkclink. Metal spout, water drop. Water drops, red glasses. Eyes hurt my eyes. Blink blink.

That mutt looks sick as hell. torn red stockings says.

Cold, my neck. Wet yellow hair red lips chew. Fweet fweet Tell us a secret. Yellow hair Skinny finger pulls. Black crosses have fingers.

Tooths show. Im bustin you out tonight, chickpea.

Red lips say, Hsst. I know you hear me.

Bright smell, shop. Wood shavings. Feed. Fweet fweet fweet birds. Bloop, bloop, fish tanks. Puppies Yip yip.

O boy. says Pretty Boyd. Rainbow wings flare.

Pink tummy cries. Pink tongue licks metal drop. Red glasses drip. Eyes hurt my eyes. My eyes water. Groan.

Brown shoes come. Mister shoes dry. Black boots wet.

Were you looking for something special, miss. says Mister. We shut soon.

Red mouth yawns. Are you a witting or witless accomplice.

Pardon.

Very clever. Long brown coat turns, boot heels clic, clic, clic. Yellow tail shivers. Cheep cheep cheep.

Tell him all that rocking is making that mutt seasick.

Swish swish. says yellow tail. Clic clac clic clac clic. say black boots. Water drops, floorboards. Jinglelee. says bell. Water drops, floorboards.

Doberman pup, green bottle fall. Pup yelps. Floorboards my tummy lies. Water drops big, my eye. Hollers come. Pretty Boyd wings flapflap Cage birds Cui cui cui Mister jumps Holy Moses what a racket Tranquille my boy Calm down Take it easy now Whats wrong.

My shoulder Hand pats. My shoulder shakes, my shoulder burns, my back Floorboards hits bam bam bam fire jumps Floorboards my hollering foots kick My head my fists hit hit hit. Fireflies spin. Hollering.

Im sorry, my boy. I forgot. Im sorry. Dont hurt yourself.

My eyes nose mouth wet. Burning. My eyes blink blink blink. My throat hurts. Mister hands show. Tranquille my boy. Mister says. I mean, theres a wonderful good boy surrounded by friends. We should like him to know he is safe.

Fire gets little. My eyes my sleeve wipes. Floorboards my tummy lies. Water drops sparkle. Sparkle my fingertips pet. Sparkly tails water drops make. My throat hurts. Byebye.

Whats got under his skin this time. says Mister. *Q*

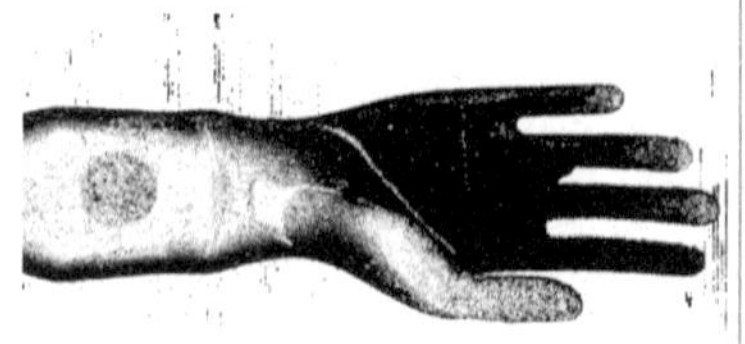

Knitting Alone For Thousands of Miles: Pens, Ink, Pencils

M. F. McAuliffe

PENS

We began to use ink in grade 3, and ink meant ink in bottles and pens with separate, curved, replaceable nibs — wooden or plastic nib-holder, steel nib — and you could get them at places like the local greengrocer, along with sheets of glittery pictures to stick into scrapbooks with glue made from flour and water .

Great varieties of nibs, fine, medium, broad — nothing as broad as an broad American calligraphic nib, nothing like; it was the kind of nib a bank-clerk would have used during the Boer War, that kind of pen-holder, also. Dipping the nib, draining it against the side of the bottle, achieving the balance (too much ink vs. having to re-dip too few letters later).

The pale aqua pen-holder that eventually got chewed so much that its point broke off – oh, how miserable it was, how unlovable, the shaft with the Mt. St. Helen-sized shear, and the balance fatally affected.

My father's pen, mid-brown wooden with the dark Quink-coloured ink-stain. I think it must have hailed from the early 40s, if not his night-classes in the late 30s.

Mapping-pens from Sands and MacDougall, Stationers, of King William Street, tiny, between a 10th and a 16th of an inch across, intimidating because Indian ink is indelible.

And the rest of the stationary store: concentrated cordial-colours of protractors and set-squares looked at edge-on; the slightly repellent light from the cheap and stiff and difficult brass compasses; the oddness of the slightly marbled plastic Australias — sometimes the same colours that laminex came in (one long wandering slit for the Murray-Darling, complete absence of other holes signifying sizeable bodies of water, the borders long, slotted lines); the unstable, toppling plastic Britains with their slotted borders, nearly snapping at Scotland.

INK

At home we used Skrip — a mid-royal blue; the bottle had a small well built into the side of the neck. You tipped the whole bottle upside down (with the cap on) and the well would fill. You used that for dipping the nib — it kept you from dipping into the bottle itself and getting ink above the metal section that held the nib (and making your pen look horrible). My father was a chartered accountant. His books were perfect: pale, marble-edged folio-sized pages, columns of copperplate words and figures in Skrip

mid-blue.

As you opened the bottle the slightly sharp smell, the deep and vivid liquid, the clear glass containments, the sense of great possibility.

The main ink favoured by the girls at school was Quink, a darker, greeney-blue ink make by the Parker company, which also made fountain-pens. Among the girls in grades 6 & 7 — the trick was to add water to the ink to make it paler. The palest ink didn't necessarily win — ink could, unbelievably, be too pale.

The worst thing you could do was use the school ink — greeney-black gunk, made at the beginning of the term out behind the tuck shop, older boys using funnels and odd rubber tubing and clear glass demijons, the green component standing thin and separate on the glass above the dark mass of the black and sedimentary sludge.

At mysteriously-determined moments the designated boys poured it — demijons from the sliding-door cupboards at the back of the room — into the black inkwells built into every desk. The inkwells were plastic, got stuffed with blotting-paper, got filthy. I think cleaning them — at the end of the term — was somebody's punishment.

Ink at highschool became Skrip in the fountain-pen (Platignum, dark goldey-black leopard-coloured stripes), replaced in Leaving by the Bic — Australian for ballpoint — you could write faster with them and you had to write fast in those hot, sweaty, mind-blank exams, 1, 2, or 3 hours, invigilated in a sandstone hall in the city.

Latin in 2nd Yr., 1963. Hot afternoons, your head nearly level with the desk while you wrote with your fountain-pen, slight smell of wet ink, hot bright green leaves through the window, and the inkstain working its way into the callous on the knuckle near the fingernail on your third finger. The callous went away only after you stopped writing all day every day. After Uni.

PENCILS

My mother always kept a Copperplate pencil on top of the penny-box by the phone in the kitchen. The pencil was perennially, unalterably, essentially, transubstantiatedly blunt. The only paper we had to hand were the rectangular, bent, sweet, waxy, recursively-scented liners from Palmolive soap. (Those dark brown, oval, translucent bars of glycerine, Pears soap, didn't have paper liners. The white wrapping was all there was. Pears was special; Pears was the soap you couldn't get during the War.)

The waxy side of a Palmolive soap liner was impervious to the very blunt pencil; the other side was not. I did pre-school doodles. My mother wrote grocery lists.

The first thing I wrote with at school was a stone stick. I wrote on a slate. We wiped the slate clean with a damp rag, waited for the surface to dry, and began again. I don't think I did this very long; my memories of this are soft and fleeting. My next firm memory is of one of the pencils my father brought home from work — another blunt point, but the lead was

a kind of redbrown brick. He brought a small pad of oddly-lined paper, too. I took it to school and used the pad and the pencil to learn addition, and also to learn that the page wasn't used up when I'd drawn a very small circle enclosing a cross in the top right-hand corner. I didn't want to go back to those pages, but did; filled them with arithmetic. 2+2=4.

Blunt. Brick. (Shouldn't be. The lines on the pad too dark, too close together blunt, shouldn't be, looming tall black shape, looming, smelling of a different kind of breakfast, yelling.)

What did we do yesterday?

That was when I began lodging knowledge in the corners of the classroom where the ceiling met the walls, finding it there the next day in my panic, in the pressure of the questions, using it to ward off the horror that followed failure to answer. What did we do yesterday? — Two and two are four. — What are two and two? — Four!

Great pencil-makers of the 1950s... Australia: Copperplate; Germany: Staedtler; England: Derwent. (Oh, those tiered rows — 72 colour-graduated Derwent pencils, how they promised to reproduce reality, make it something you could take with you in your pocket and have — How I wanted one of those boxes. How vastly it would have been wasted on someone who still can't draw...) My cousin mentioned recently that you couldn't reproduce a South Australian sky with Derwent colours. (Oh... Of course. They match the English landscape.)

Staedtler pencils had a profile of a Spartan soldier in a helmet near the top of the shaft. They seemed very stately. Copperplate pencils were pointed; the pointed end was painted black, separated from the thinner red paint on the shaft by a thin white stripe. The pencils were hexagonal; comforting to run along your lips in moments of happy inattention, chunky and satisfying when chewing your pencil was all the protest you could make. *Q*

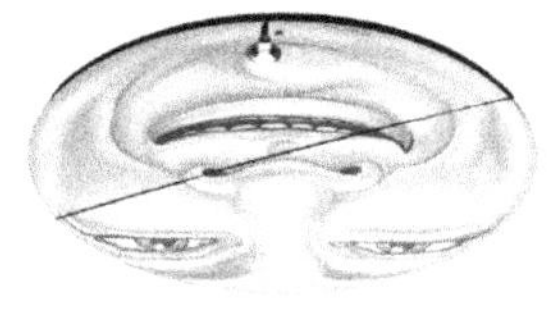

MESO provides capital, coaching, and comprehensive support to entrepreneurs in Washington, Clackamas, Multnomah and Columbia counties of Oregon.

MESO's mission is to improve the economic opportunities of underserved individuals through empowerment, education, entrepreneurship for the benefit of greater community.

Contact MESO for support in growing your business!

Portland: 503-841-3351
4008 NE Martin Luther King Jr Blvd., Portland, OR 97212

Beaverton: 503-521-7620
12525 SW 3rd Street, Beaverton, OR 97005

St. Helens: Wauna Federal Credit Union via 503-841-3351

Rhode Island, via N.Y.C.

Who Doesn't Know Murphy's Law?

Priscilla Galligan

Who doesn't know Murphy's law?

"If anything can go wrong, it will." Always would, could. Still will.

I work in health care, a nursing and rehabilitative care center.

Sounds nice, yes?

Make the best of a waiting-patiently-to-die situation: many activities: rehab, bingo; speech, physical and occupational therapy, arts and crafts. Musical entertainment with Jacques' accordion every Friday after the fish pie luncheon special.

Let me introduce the infamous Wayne John. Now, that's a name for a player — retired cruise ship director, self-proclaimed international playboy. The bed hopper of Summer Glen Rehab — here for restorative care following a stroke — resident social butterfly, bed-hopper, sergeant, ret. (Army), and cruise ship director. He has a penchant for older women, and due to his cognitive deficits — amnesia mostly — he cannot distinguish the comatose from the coherent. A sad case, indeed.

But he has lots of fun while the nurses and nurses' aides keep busy with their assignments, lights buzzing. He always offers to pass out the coffee on morning shift with donuts and magazines, and then, at 8 p.m., assorted beverages and a whirlwind of cookies and other special treats he should not deliver. Sometimes he passes out slices of the cake his daughter brings him on Sunday (a kind of place card in their relationship); sweetness achieved in angel food bundt cake with no chocolate. He takes this seriously, makes the women swoon with his questions, pleas for validation, praise for a good job well done.

Snack time.

He is attentive in setting up this med cart used by the day nurses for suction machines, IV pumps, treatments for necrotic tissue, and catheter insertion. Tonight his cart is proud, exhuberant: washed with alcohol, clothed with tablecloth, holiday prep trays from the kitchen, cookies, juices, teas, milk, and ice creams.

What is he living for? A quiet room and a tender glance. Rose's room.

Rose is the night owl. Always awake, swearing those 40 words the FCC ruled off radio, insisting night after night one of her relatives is coming *To take me outta this dump!*

This winter's Thursday we are understaffed and no one pays much attention to snack trays and the pleading of women called Rose. He makes his way into her room to bring: a smile, cranberry juice, and four packs of Lorna Doone shortbread cookies.

She smiles, thanks him, and the fire alarms go off in his head and the hallway. They are in Rose's room and he cannot leave.

Rose says okay, I have to lie down, make yourself at home until the alarm's cleared.

He makes his way over to her bed, so fast, and turns her around, kisses, fast, pulls

up her nightie, pushing her onto the bed as he covers her shock with his hand on her mouth, her eyes staring deep into his, and he and she are as one. It lasts 14 minutes.

More than Stan ever could muster, Rose thinks to herself. And then, when the act is over, he is stuck. Not as in love-struck stuck; stuck like a badly behaved animal.

She snickers at him in her disapproval ("*Tsk-tsk-tsk*"), leans her left hand over to the nightstand and calls 911.

Wayne John (his real name) blushes. Rose continues to slap him as they ride the stretcher into the ambulance together. *Q*

For A Living

Do gloves really wait for hands?
Or are they most at home
Forgotten on a closet shelf or
Balled into a pocket

There with a friend
Bearing coffee stains and frayed stitching
As a badge of honor
They can engage in a life of quiet contemplation

Part Buddhist, part mushroom
Growing in self awareness
With each under-utilized moment
Until they are called upon to do their job

All the past
Conveniently forgotten

— *Michael Shay*

Little Beirut, Oregon

Actual Poem

Suddenly it is quiet suddenly.
I want to lie down on your lawn
Your parking strip
Among decades of chemicals
The kinds that make things green
And suck up these stars
Through a tiny pink straw,
Like bubbles

— *Tiffany Lee Brown*

The Greatest Famine in History

labor camps posted as communes — slave labor,
occupation, so mao said they have too much food. he
shut the canteens, cut off noses for harvesting the harvest.

steal food, even unripe, time and again they will.
I can't stand the houses, he said. chinese architecture
is most delightful when torn to the ground like this, and
he snapped and tanks shot concrete like semen

impregnating the concrete with more concrete
as people starved in the city, and nationwide, said
a famine witness in Peking, dejection in each county,
each village, each home where all the children died

eating pond scum, needing rice. aesthetics.
this is why they died, just as the mao souvenir
alarm clock will never tell time, engineered
wrong on purpose. tens of millions of people.

— *Dena Rash Guzman*

Щербина ЛИМЕРИКИ

Родившись, Борис Пастернак
был косноязычен и наг.
Подрос, огляделся,
слегка приоделся
и стал сексуальный маньяк.

У Анны Андревны Ахматовой
был в детстве котенок лохматовый.
Котенка не жаль, пошел он на шаль
на плечи великой Ахматовой.

Какая противная рожа, —
со скукой подумал Сережа.
Той рожей был Ленин.
Сережей – Есенин,
и были они непохожи.

Однажды в Шахматово Блок
Вел с мамой такой диалог:
Хочу быть юристом,
Хочу быть артистом!
- Да ты ж не отличник, милок.

За ней он ходил по пятам.
Она говорила: не дам.
Она говорила, она повторила:
«Настырный же Вы, Мандельштам».

Однажды по привычке идиотской
стал сочинять стихи Иосиф Бродский.
И написал опять
ну гениально, блядь,
и так писал всегда Иосиф Бродский.

— Щербина, 1980

ŠČERBINA LIMERICKS

At birth, Boris Pasternak
was vocal and buck naked.
He sprouted, looked around,
put on a bespoke tux and
turned into a sexual maniac.

Anna Andreevna Akhmatova
in childhood had a fury kitten.
A cat aught not be pitied that pawed
the shawl on the shoulders of a giant.

Oh, what a despicable mug —
thought Sergey, bored and smug.
The mug belonged to Lenin.
And Sergey, that was Esenin.
They resembled each other not.

Once at their dacha Blok
And his mother dialoged:
I want to become a jurist,
I want to become an artist!
You're no A-student, lug.

He followed on her heels like a pup
But she told him: I will not shtup.
She said it once, and then "Oh, damn!
You're so persistent, Mandelstam"

Under the spell of bad habit once
Joseph Brodsky began to compose lines.
And surely enough he did scribe,
a fuckin' genius! brilliant as
ever Joseph Brodsky's writing was.

— Transl., Alexander Cigale

Ouija Board: A comic by Sarah Laing

OH, YOU'RE DOING A OUIJA BOARD, ARE YOU? THOSE THINGS ARE A CROCK.

IF THEY'RE A CROCK THEN WHY ARE YOU HERE?
ME, I NEVER REST. PEOPLE ARE ALWAYS RAKING MY ASHES.

I MEAN, REALLY, HOW MANY BIOGRAPHIES DO THEY NEED ABOUT ME? THEY'LL NEVER GET IT RIGHT ANYWAY. IT'S ALL JACK'S FAULT—HE SHOULD'VE BURNT MY LETTERS LIKE I TOL HM TO.

SO DOES THAT MEAN YOU DON'T WANT ME WRITING A GRAPHIC NOVEL ABOUT YOU?
WHAT CHOICE DO I HAVE IN THE MATTER? I'M DEAD REMEMBER

BUT YES, IF PRESSED, I WOULD'VE CHOSEN SOMEONE ELSE TO DO IT. DYLAN HORROCKS IS A BETTER DRAWER THAN YOU... AND KATE BEATON IS BETTER AT THE FUNNY HISTORICAL STUFF. MARY & BRYAN TALBOT, NOW THEY DID A GREAT BIO OF JAMES JOYCE'S DAUGHTER

AND ALISON BECHDEL IS REALLY SMART & SHE HAS A GREAT UNDERSTAND-ING OF MODERNIST LITERATURE THANKS TO ALL THOSE BOOKS HER DAD LEFT HER TO READ...

BUT THEY DON'T WANT TO WRITE A GRAPHIC NOVEL ABOUT YOU.
SIGH YES, I'M STUCK WITH YOU, A WOMAN OF MODEST LITERARY TALENT & DUBIOUS DRAWING SKILLS.
AND I DON'T HAVE TO WRITE ABOUT YOU. I HAVE OTHER IDEAS YOU KNOW. SHORT STORIES—
SHORT STORIES— PSHAW— YOU'RE STILL USING THE SAME TRICKS I TAUGHT YOU IN THE EARLY 20TH CENTURY.
CIGARETTE?
I DON'T SMOKE.
GHOST CIGARETTES CAN'T GIVE YOU CANCER.
OH, ALRIGHT THEN.
I USED TO DABBLE IN THE OCCULT IN THE BAD OLD DAYS.
COUGH ALEISTER CROWLEY, RIGHT?
NOW HE WAS A CURIOUS MAN, FILTHY RICH AND MAD AS A SNAKE OF COURSE. I WENT AROUND TO HIS HOUSE TO TAKE PART IN ONE OF HIS RITUALS...
SMOKE THIS, MY DEAR, IF YOU WISH FOR ENLIGHTENMENT.

motherfoucault's
523 SE Morrison St.
Portland, OR 97214
503 236 - 2665
books

silentarmy.org
COMIC ART COLLECTIVE
SINCE 2002

Her Camera

She brought her camera
to the underworld
where she journeyed to retrieve
the parts of her lover's body.

She had not thought of
the faces of the dead,
she had not wondered who
would perform the tortures,

the same sick devils who hauled
manure, to dance and drink
and puke and brawl in the dust
the night before the Sabbath.

The same film that showed
the dead face of the Ice Man
also revealed the tormenters,
the half-men who had been whole

when the world was young.
In the world of dust and waste
she also saw her own face,
her thumb raised in a cheerful salute.

Surely everybody knows
that the underworld is our own,
everybody knows the dust
is our own dust,

the rusty key is to our own doors
and Orpheus will never return.

— *Douglas Spangle*

SIE LANGWEILTE SICH

Die Straßen waren ihr zu wenig fremd,
die Restaurants und Kinos kamen ihr
vor, so, als wollten sie ihr lästig fallen,
nicht müde war sie worden, nein, nur kalt,
eine Gleichgült'ge ging sie neben Menschen
und Wagen hin, Neues war nicht vorhanden,
die Herrenwelt zum Beispiel schien ihr alt,
junge und fröhl'che Leute machten ein
Gesicht, benahmen sich auf eine Weise,
daß sie den Gipfel der Unint'ressantheit
darstellten. Kokettieren lohnte sich
nicht mehr. «Langweilig ist mein Aufenthalt
in dieser einst für mich so hübschen Stadt
geworden», sprach sie zu sich selber. Täglich
dacht' sie dasselbe, wünschte sich genötigt,
zu reisen und doch liebt' sie das Verschmähte,
fand im Verachteten noch immer viel
Schönes, blieb nicht und ging nicht fort und sah
sich
vertrieben und doch wieder angezogen
vom scheinbar schon zu lang Vertrauten,
fragend die Menschen ihr ins Antlitz schauten.

— *Robert Walser*

TRÜBER NACHBAR

Es liegt schon da wie ein anderes Haus,
doch dringt den ganzen Tag hinaus
das Schreien armer Kinder.
Die Kinder der «bessern» Leute sind
geschwind beim Ohrläppchen gefaßt, geschwind,
die der Armen noch zweimal geschwinder.
O daß zu Not und Mangel muß
auch noch Gehässigkeit setzen den Fuß,
und daß der Haß zuvor
sich alle Armen zum Opfer erkor.

Es liegt schon da wie ein anderes Haus,
doch dringt den ganzen Tag hinaus
das Weinen armer Kinder.

— *Robert Walser*

SHE WAS BORED

The streets were not strange enough
to her, the restaurants and cinemas
appeared as if they wanted to bother her,
she didn't grow tired, no, just cold,
an indifference, she walked beside people
and cars, there was nothing new, the world
of gentlemen, for example, seemed old,
young and happy people made a face,
behaved in such a way, they represented
the height of uninterestingness. Flirting
wasn't worth it anymore. "Bored is now
my stay in this city that was once
so beautiful to me," she told herself.
Every day she thought the same,
wished she were forced to travel,
yet she loved the despised, still
found much that was beautiful
in her scorn, didn't stay and didn't leave
and saw herself banished yet attracted
by that which had seemed familiar for too
long, questioning, the people faced her.

— *Trans., Daniele Pantano*

GLOOMY NEIGHBOR

It does sit there like another house,
but all day long the screaming
of poor children leaks out.
The children of "better" people
are seized promptly by the ears, promptly,
and the ones of the poor twice as fast.
Oh that spite must now add
its foot to misery and despair,
that all the poor have already
been chosen as hate's first victims.

It does sit there like another house,
but all day long the crying
of poor children leaks out.

— *Trans., Daniele Pantano*

SONGS FROM THE SICKBED

(i.)

Poems from the Sickbed

A skeleton curves
Against flash-white pillows.
The only thing between skin and a stain
Is the blood.

(ii.)

The Sore Throat

A long trail of mucus seeps through us.
Quiet, we mustn't speak when what we want is
Song.

(iii.)

At the Hostel

On rented sheets I smooshed a tick
Or what I thought was a tick, full and red
That left a bloodstain on the yellow duvet.
The Lover
Has a scar on his forehead
That came from a nourishment tube because he was born
Six months premature.
He has been to Africa
Where he worked with AIDS patients
And does not believe in a God.
I fake sickness to leave while he is still asleep. I can not stand it when
he touches my arms.

— *Monica Storss*

SUNDAY

I sweep scarlet leaves
into piles that you gather
in silent sunlight.

— *Wendy Chin-Tanner*

FULL MOON

The moon sets the birds to chirping at three,
there, sitting high above the trees,

a rolled back eyeball showing its white,
shining on and on, its brightness, its light

buzzing, singing, Don't sleep! Don't sleep!
How little you matter. How little you keep.

— *Wendy Chin-Tanner*

Portfolio / Wedding Dance, photography, M. F. McAuliffe

Les Mots I

Les mots   je le sais maintenant   déclamaient du vent à
  l'époque
à part les cailloux il y avait des lunes mais pas de lampes
les étoiles sortirent plus tard d'une empoignade entre deux
  silex

Cinq cailloux pour tour vous dire
un par continent
assez vaste   pour contenir un enfant de couleur différente

Il y avait donc   cinq enfants mais pas de maisons
des fenêtres mais pas de murs
du vent mais pas de rues
le premier homme portrait une pierre autour du cou

Il fit un arrangement avec le premier arbre
un chêne si mes souvenirs sont bons
celui qui arrivait avant l'autre buvait l'océan

Le langage en ce temps-là était une ligne droite réservée
  aux oiseaux
la lettre « i » fente de colibri femelle
« h » échelle à une seule marche nécessaire pour remplacer
  avant la nuit un soleil grillé
« o » trou dans la semelle de l'univers

Contrairement aux consonnes aux vêtements rêches
les voyelles étaient nues
tout l'art du tissage consistait à ménager leur susceptibilité
le soir elles se comptaient entre elles pour s'assurer
  qu'aucune ne manquait
dans les pays caillouteux les hommes avaient un sommeil
  sans rêves

— *Vénus Khoury-Ghata*

Words I

In those days   I know now   words declaimed the wind
besides pebbles, there were moons, but no lamps
the stars would emerge later from a brawl between two flintstones

I'll tell you everything   there were five pebbles
one for each continent
vast enough   to contain a child of a different color

So there were   five children but no houses
windows but no walls
wind but no streets
the first man wore a stone around his neck

He made an arrangement with the first tree
an oak if I remember correctly
the one who got there first could drink up the ocean

Language at that time was a straight line reserved for birds
the letter "i" was the cleft of a female hummingbird
"h" a ladder with one rung necessary to replace a charred sun before nightfall
"o" a hole in the sole of the universe

Unlike the consonants with their rough garments
the vowels were naked
all the weaver's art consisted of humoring them
in the evening they counted each other to make sure no one was missing
in the rocky countries men slept without dreaming

— *Trans., Marilyn Hacker*

The Pet Thief (Two)

Kassten Alonso

Psst. Oboy.

My bent knee on stone windowsill. Window sash my dirty fingers hold. Down my shoulder, in courtyard, little Freda stands. Kick kick Bunny brown coatsleeve hugs. Yellow Freda hair shines in lamplight. Freda eyes bingbing.

Freda finger lifts. Shadow moves on stones. Freda hisses, See that. Hanging from that balcony up there. Up there. Dont stare at my finger. Look, upstairs there, the balcony. See. The savonnerie. The rug. I want it.

Window. Green blinds. Snoring Macaw hides.

No bird tonight, Oboy. Freda voice hisses. No bird. Non. Non. Non. Non. The rug. Get the rug.

Window dirty fingers shut. Collar tag clink clink. Stones Hands grab. From sill knee slides, to stone moulding foot goes. Stone joints fingertips grip. Bent corner, drainpipe, come. Drainpipe my hands pull Stones my foots climb. Shadows on stones. My foot steps, my foot steps to windowsill. Tippy toe balcony. Rug hangs. My arm lifts, fingers flutter. Bracelet jimmy shines on my wrist. Rug fingers scratch. Bunny cries.

In courtyard, in lamplight, yellow Freda hair flaps sidetoside. Bunny arm waves, legs kick, fussy. Sh sh sh sh. Freda says. Bunny Freda hip bounces, Sh sh sh sh. Eyes shine on my eyes, blinkblink. Metal tags clink clink.

Hurry, Oboy. Bunnys going to wake the natives.

Knees bend, legs jump, to hand balcony grate comes. Balcony squeaks. Little courtyard rocks sidetoside. Fingers hurt, arm swings Rug Hand slaps Rug goes. My shoulder pulls fingers Grate hurts. My hanging legs swing, twist.

Quit monkeying around, Tarzan. Freda hisses.

My legs swing, dirty foots stones hit, push, arm swings, rug hand grabs, Rug says shhhhhtwap From my fingers Rug pulls whoowhoowhoo falls Jesus jumping Freda hollers, lamplight shadows swing Bunny Brown coatsleeve hugs Stones Rug slaps.

Shoulder elbow fingers hurt. Arm lifts, to fingers grate comes. For downstairs windowsill Tootsies kick. Legs swing, swing, swing, Grate Hands let go Foots stone windowsill hits Knees spakspak window Dripcap stones Fingernails scratch, catch.

Breath comes, breath goes.

To rug little clic clac Freda walks. Freda says, Remind me not to take any magic carpet rides with you, swami.

Black pants kneels. Bunny Freda hands sits on stones. Stones little hands hit hit, fussy Reeeooo. Shadow bounce in lamplight.

Rug Freda hands roll. Roll gets big. Freda rises, hands clap, black boot on

roll. Come on, lets go. says Freda. Pale forehead lifts, eyes pingping, mouth opens. O, bloody hell. Freda hollers, Beware the Irish confetti.

Windowsill Onion hits My heel twists Onion skips off stone wall to courtyard, bounces.

Ma savonnerie. balcony says. Thieves.

Fat green sweater sleeve on balcony railing. Vegetables green sleeve holds to big tummy. Grey hair, glasses shine. Gypsy scum, stealing from a poor god-fearing old woman. glittery glasses say.

Tomato flies Splat My hair, my forehead my eyes Wet sprays. Drainpipe my hands grab. My shoulder Lettuce head hits leaves burst shadows leaves flutter, fall.

High window hollers, Ils volent la couverture de Madame Chuvot.

Courtyard hollers, Bastardes. Stealing poor old womans prize heirloom. And you bring your baby to your crime, for what, to riun her by yuor werchted wyas you dnemad foilosh gsyipes.

Trembly cucumber Wrinkly balcony hand shows. Rattly drainpipe my falling hands clap clap clap, my dirty foots stones scrape, falling shadows swing sidetoside. Drainpipe Cucumber hits bang cucumber bounces off my coatsleeve, falls to courtyard.

Windows get bright, sashes squeal grumble groan courtyard door opens striped pajamas holler, Arrêtez.

Non, Emile. They always carry knives.

Drainpipe flies Stones leap hit my foots My hands stones slap slap. Dirt, straw, seeds, burnt broke cigarettes, bones. Tomato hits, busts.

Rug Freda boot kicks. Pick it up Oboy allons y. Rug my hands lift. Bunny Freda hands lift, tsokk tsokk tsokk black boots run In brown coatsleeve Bunny bounces twinkles haw haw haw haw Rug my arms hug, my hip rug bounces, rug flops, brushes running stones. Stones carrots hit, tumble.

Basement window hollers, Gspyy trsah, you oghut to be steond to dateh.

Apple, can, parsnip, pan, cabbage, potpie, artichoke fly, bounce clatter spin, stones. Freda caws, boots run tsokk tsokk tsokka tsokk Bunny bounces, in brown coatsleeve twinkles In my arms rug bounces, rubs my hip, rug dips Rug Hands knee swing to shoulder Rug smells smoky skin mold dust Lip curls throats shut Arm hugs rug shoulder Black Freda boots tsokka tsokka tsokk corner, byebye, down crinkle crankle curvy stone walls, torn coloured papers, skinky trees, collar tag tinkles, triptrap bridge shiny dark canal whispers, spills, dizzies me.

White pickets. White pickets comes. Dollhouse. Gate Black boot kicks Clap Freda runs Bunny bounces, Ivy ruffles pink Bunny hat, Bunny eyes on my eyes, brown coat shoulder Darkness hides. Black Freda boots say clacclac up steps in shop, in darkness.

Gate my hip bumps Hand Ivy scratches rug Darkness up steps my foots thup thup thup, Freda bootprints glow in darkness. On steps, cat eyes blinkblink. Manx hisses.

Tippy top stairs, doorway, candlelight flickers. In cages birds brrr birds awk birds cui cui cui cui. On mattress Freda lies, hahahaha. Bunny Freda hands squeeze. Bunny Freda arms shake, Bunny twinkles. Little Bunny FooFoo did you regardes le visage de vieille when she caught your papa stealing her rug. Did you see the look on your papas face. Have you ever seen your papa get hit by a bloody tomato before.

To Freda mouth Bunny falls on round Bunny cheek Ribbet Ribbet Bunny twinkles wheeeee legs kick Bunny Freda hands fly to mattress Freda rolls to floorboards Freda rises. Brown coat shakes skinny shoulders show Coat Black sweater sleeve on floorboards throws. Black sweater sleeves Hands push. Pale arms, candlelight.

Okay, lets unfurl Madame Chuvots priceless objet de famille. Rug Freda hands pull Hollers come Let go, Oboy, off my shoulder rug falls to wood floorboards. Dust paffs in trembly candlelight in cages hollering Greenyellowbluewhite wings flapflapflap. To floorboards Sofa tabby leaps, darting tail. To my botty Mattress comes. Bunny my hands take. Bunny mouth open, grey eyes on my eyes. My collar tag Bunny fingers pull. Papa. Black Bunny hair My fingers scratch.

Bunny twinkles. Cage bars Blue parakeet gnaws.

Plastic cups, cream cups, black Freda boots kick, wrappers, books, newspaper, shoes, soda can, clothing, pizza box. From cold silver radiator purring grey longhair comes.

Creeammm. grey longhair says, green eyes on my eyes, my knee fluffy paw pets.

In coat pocket my hand fumbles cream cup. Cup shows. Cup cooing Bunny fingers grab. Cup my fingers take from Bunny, tear off lid. Cream Furry red tongue laps from cup, grey ears twitch. Bunny fusses, little hands grab. My lap dirty Bunny booties kick.

Rug Black Freda boot kick, kick, kicks. Rug goes flat on wood floorboards. In cage Brer Rabbit twitches pink nose.

Grey longhair sits. Fluffy paw Red tongue licks, whiskers paw rubs, eyes shut, purrs. Torn cream cup Bunny hands take. Cup Bunny mouth tastes. Bunny fusses, cup little hands throw pinkle pinkle.

On books Wood icebox stands. Icebox hides ice block, milk carton, cream cups, sardine tins, yellow cheese, prosciutto, halfnhalf, salami, plastic bottle. Milk. Plastic milk bottle Hand holds to little Bunny lips. My fingers little pink fingers squeeze. Bunny mouth sucks. Bunny heavy in my arm.

Time for night night. says green parrotlet.

Corner of rug Pale Freda fingers grab on wood floorboards rug slides shhht. Grey longhair ears twitch, in silver radiator longhair hides.

This is the spot. says Freda.

Rug Turning black boots stomp, hips pale hands grab, yellow hair hangs, hips shoulders Freda turns, boots stomp. Whiteblack comes prip prip prip to rug.

Hsst. Freda hisses. Whiteblack skips turns to kitchen Darkness in doorway Eyes flash pingpingping. Bottle Bunny mouth sucks.

This rugs perfect. Freda says. It makes our darling Dollhouse top of rome. It really sets off the peeling moldy wallpaper and wet cracks in the ceiling. Seriously, though, if we had some fresh paint, and some decent furniture and window treatments and electricity and running water and heat and social status and love, and, uh, and. Blue eyes on my eyes. Tooths show in candlelight.

Look at me, Oboy. Freda says. Im nesting. Q

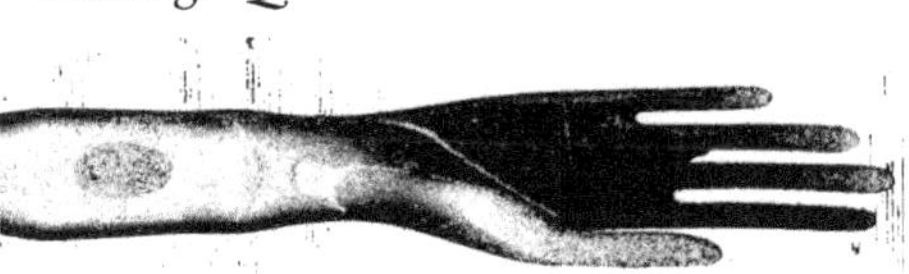

www.ingramcontent.com/pod-product-compliance
Lightning Source LLC
Chambersburg PA
CBHW071010120726
47910CB00004B/1462

* 9 7 8 1 6 3 0 6 8 1 3 9 5 *